THE

LIGHT

OF

LIFE

THE LIGHT OF LIFE

BARBARA MONTERROSA

WINTERS

Published by Winters Publishing, LLC
2448 E. 81st St. Suite #4802 | Tulsa, Oklahoma 74137 USA

Book design copyright © 2015 by Winters Publishing, LLC. All rights reserved.
Cover design by Samson Lim; revised cover ©2017 by Kristen Polson
Interior design by Jomar Ouano

Published in the United States of America

ISBN: 978-1-94772-694-8
Religion / Christian Life / Spiritual Growth
15.04.17

Contents

1

A Light Shines

The entrance of Your words gives light; it gives understanding to the simple.

—Psalm 119:130 (NKJV)

Do you know that all of creation exists because God spoke it into being? Do you know that His words are alive and powerful and carry out His purposes? Do you know that when He speaks, His words are going to become all that He has planned? It's true. In the Holy Bible, in the book of Genesis chapter 1, the words, "And God said," are completed with, "and it was so."

Whatever God said became all that He said it would be.

It is in this first chapter of Genesis that we learn the story of His creation. We learn that His words are words of life, words of purpose, and they are powerful.

> For the word of God is living and powerful, and sharper than any two-edged sword, piercing even to the division of soul and spirit, and of joints and marrow, and is a discerner of the thoughts and intents of the heart. (Hebrews 4:12, NKJV)

> So shall My word be that goes forth from My mouth; It shall not return to Me void, But it shall accomplish what I please, and it shall prosper in the thing for which I sent it. (Isaiah 55:11, NKJV)

When God had you in mind, He spoke; and you became and will become. The understanding of this is very important. See, you became when God spoke. Became is the past tense of become. That means you became what God had in mind; "You became." What God had in mind was done well. It was completed with skill and professionalism, and it was finished in His eyes.

So you became and will become. Now *become* is like the caterpillar to become a butterfly. The caterpillar *became* a caterpillar to *become* a butterfly. When God made the caterpillar, He already saw the butterfly. If we didn't know the process that the butterfly goes through, we wouldn't be able to just see a caterpillar turn into a butterfly, but God was able to do exactly that!

He knew the caterpillar had to go through metamorphosis to become the butterfly that He destined him to be! We know it is a process, which will come to be. God has a process, which will change us or develop us into something He said. Having a handful of various seeds in your hand, no one could tell what the seeds were unless they see the manifestation of them come to pass. On the other hand, having seen the fruits of each seed, we can explore its fruits and identify each seed's belonging.

You became and will become! Whatever God said about you is what you shall become because when God says it, it is what He said it to be. Whatever is happening in your life, just know that it is His purpose that will prevail. God made a plan for your life when He made you, and the plans for your life have to be aligned with His will because He made you for a greater purpose. You will become all that He said you would, because He said so.

> Remember the former things, those of long ago; I am God, and there is no other; I am God and there is none like me. I make known the end from the beginning, from ancient times, what is still to come. I say; My purpose will stand, and I will do all that I please. From the east I summon a bird of prey; from a far-off land, a man to fulfill my purpose. What I have said, that will I bring about; what I have planned, that will I do. (Isaiah 46:9–11 NIV)

> Many are the plans in a person's heart, but it is the Lord's purpose that prevails. (Proverbs 19:21 NIV)

Now the first thing that God spoke into being was the light. Then God divided the light from the darkness. It is important for us to understand that light was divided from the darkness.

God saw that the light was good, and notice, that He *separated* it from the darkness. They have separate purposes; one was to be the day, the other night.

> And God said, let there be light, and there was light. And God saw the light, that it was good; and God

divided the light from the darkness. And God called the light day and the darkness He called night. And the evening and the morning were the first day. (Genesis 1:3–5 KJV)

We recognize that the light is good from creation because God created it and saw that it was good. So light usually connotes goodness. God gave light in the form of the sun, the moon, and the stars. These lights are to rule over the day and the night and divide the light from the darkness. The sun was the greater light that God made. It is to rule over the day.

And God said, let there be lights in the firmament of the heavens to divide the day from the night; and let them be for signs, and for seasons, and for days, and years: And let them be for lights in the firmament of the heaven to give light upon the earth: and it was so. And God made two great lights, the greater light to rule the day, and the lesser light to rule the night: He made the stars also. And God set them in the firmament of the heaven to give light upon the earth, and to rule over the day and over the night, and to divide the light from the darkness: and God saw that it was good. (Genesis 1:14–18 KJV)

To Him who made great lights, for His mercy endures forever-The sun to rule by day, For His mercy endures forever; the moon and stars to rule by night, for His mercy endures forever. (Psalm 136:7–9, NKJV)

The sun would be a greater light upon the earth, the brighter light in order for us to see. The sun also warms the earth; the heat and light is necessary for life on planet earth. We understand also that plants turn toward the light. The sun gives the light necessary for plants to grow and live. Even we humans find ourselves being drawn toward the light. We use the sun's light to help us live and grow. It is important that we understand the difference between the physical light and the spiritual light. *However, the spiritual is not first, but the natural, and afterward the spiritual.* (1 Corinthians 15:46, NKJV)

The Great Light, the True Light

Notice that in Genesis 1:15, 17, both verses say, "to give light upon the earth." This is important so we truly know God bestowed upon the earth the natural light. And we know that from the scriptures that God gave the greater light to rule the day as we know it to be the sun. But did you also know that God gave us another great light— the true and the greatest light of the world? It did not come from the greater light, the sun, in fact, it existed before the sun was made. Now you might be thinking, what is this other great light?

First of all, God is Spirit /Invisible, and also God is three in one—the Father, the Word, and the Holy Spirit. The name of the Godhead is "Lord Jesus Christ."

> "God is Spirit, and those who worship Him must worship in spirit and truth." (John 4:24, NKJV)

> Now to the King eternal, immortal, invisible, to God who alone is wise, be honor and glory forever and ever. Amen. (1 Timothy 1:17, NKJV)

For there are three that bear witness in heaven: the Father, the Word, and the Holy Spirit; and these three are one. (1 John 5:7, NKJV)

In the beginning was the Word, and the Word was with God, and the Word was God. He was in the beginning with God. All things were made through Him, and without Him nothing was made that was made. (John 1:1–3, NKJV)

Jesus Christ is the image of the invisible God. If you notice in the scriptures, God refers to Himself often as: *Us, We,* and *Our.* According to Gen. 1:26 (NKJV), God said, "Let Us make man in Our image, according to Our likeness; In verse 27 (NKJV), "So God created man in His own image; in the image of God He created him; 1 John 5:7 tells us that the Father, the Word, and the Holy Spirit are one. When Adam and Eve sinned against God, God said, "Behold the man has become like one of Us, to know good and evil. (Gen. 3:22, NKJV)

In John 14:23 Jesus said We will come to him and make Our home with him.

But it is in John 17:21–23, 26 that Jesus explains it best.

"That they all may be one, as *You, Father, are in Me, and I in You*; that they also may be one in Us, that the world may believe that You sent Me. "And the glory which You gave Me I have given them, that they may be one *just as We are one*: "I in them, and You in Me; that they may be made perfect in one, and that the world may know that You have sent Me, and have loved them as You have loved Me. "And I have declared to them Your name, and will declare it, that the love with which You loved Me may be in them, and I in them." (John 17:21–23, 26, NKJV;)

Jesus answered and said to him, "If anyone loves Me, he will keep My word; and My Father will love him, and We will come to him and make Our home with him. (John 14:23, NKJV)

Now what is this other great light?

Life is seeing the light not because of the sun, but because of the Son.

Adam and Eve were the first people that God created. I'm sure that the first great light they saw was not only when they looked up at the sun, but also when they lifted their heads up to the Son who created them. Adam and Eve saw the great light from the sun as we do. I believe that the sun was not the only great light to them, but the Son was the greatest light to them. Why might I be thinking this? Well, just as I said earlier, truly God gave the sun for light upon the earth for us, but also He gave His Son to be the true light of the world, and the greatest light.

Now you might be thinking, wasn't God's Son not born until the New Testament, and just about 2,000 years ago? How then could Jesus be the true and greatest light to Adam and Eve and have created them? The Jews did not understand when Jesus spoke to them that He was before their Father Abraham and the prophets. They asked Jesus who He was making Himself out to be. We know that from the scriptures that Jesus was born into the world after Abraham, but He was already *before* Abraham.

The Jews did not understand this.

"Are You greater than our father Abraham, who is dead? And the prophets are dead. Who do You make Yourself out to be?"

Jesus answered, "If I honor Myself, My honor is nothing. It is My Father who honors Me, of whom you say that He is your God. "Yet you have not known Him, but I know Him. And if I say, 'I do not know Him,' I shall be a liar like you; but I do know Him and keep His word. Your father Abraham rejoiced to see My day, and he saw it and was glad."

Then the Jews said to Him, "You are not yet fifty years old, and have You seen Abraham?"

Jesus said to them, "Most assuredly, I say to you, before Abraham was, I AM." (John 8:53–58, NKJV)

John the Baptist knew this truth as he came to bear witness of Jesus the True Light.

John bore witness of Him and cried out, saying, "This was He of whom I said, 'He who comes after me is preferred before me, for He was before me.'" (John 1:15, NKJV)

"This is He of whom I said, 'After me comes a Man who is preferred before me, for He was before me.' (John 1:30, NKJV)

See, the scriptures tell us that John the Baptist was also born before Jesus, and still, John knew that Jesus was before him. John the Baptist also knew that Jesus was the light.

This man came for a witness, to bear witness of the Light, that all through him might believe. He was

not that Light, but was sent to bear witness of that
Light. (John 1:7–8, NKJV)

See John the Baptist came to bear witness to Jesus the
Light. A man named Simeon also spoke about Jesus the
Light. Simeon says that Jesus is a light to bring revelation
to the Gentiles.

> And behold, there was a man in Jerusalem whose
> name was Simeon, and this man was just and
> devout, waiting for the Consolation of Israel, and
> the Holy Spirit was upon him.
> And it had been revealed to him by the Holy
> Spirit that he would not see death before he had
> seen the Lord's Christ. (Luke 2:25–26, NKJV)

> "Lord, now You are letting Your servant depart in
> peace, According to Your word; For my eyes have
> seen Your salvation Which You have prepared before
> the face of all peoples, a light to bring revelation to
> the Gentiles, and the glory of Your people Israel."
>
> (Luke 2: 29-32, NKJV)

We must know that in the beginning, even before God
created the heaven and the earth, and before God spoke
the creation of light into being, God's Word was the light
of life already. In fact, the Holy Bible says the Word of God
was already in the beginning. His name is called The Word
of God. Who is the Word? Jesus!

The Word is what created it all in the beginning; God
spoke, and His Word created. And also remember that in
the scriptures God refers to Himself often as *Us, We,* and
Our, and the three are one.

In the beginning was the Word, and the Word was with God, and the Word was God. He was in the beginning with God. All things were made through Him, and without Him nothing was made that was made. (John 1:1–3, NKJV)

He is the image of the invisible God, the firstborn over all creation. For by Him all things were created that are in heaven and that are on earth, visible and invisible, whether thrones or dominions or principalities or powers. All things were created through Him and for Him. And He is before all things, and in Him all things consist. (Colossians 1:15–17, NKJV)

He was clothed with a robe dipped in blood, and His name is called The Word of God. (Revelation 19:13, NKJV)

"You are worthy, O Lord, To receive glory and honor and power; For You created all things, And by Your will they exist and were created." (Revelation 4:11, NKJV)

For there are three that bear witness in heaven: the Father, the Word, and the Holy Spirit; and these three are one. (1 John 5:7, NKJV)

"Let not your heart be troubled; you believe in God, believe also in Me. (John 14:1, NKJV)

John 1:1–3 tells us that in the beginning, the Word (Jesus) was with God, and He was God. 1 John 1:5 also tells us that God is light. Knowing this truth, when Adam and Eve's eyes were first opened I believe they seen the greatest light, who is the Word of God. Imagine just being created out of the dust from the ground, and God breathing into your nostrils—the breath of life; and you became a living being just as Adam was. Imagine opening your eyes for the first time and being the only one around, what do you then suppose would be the greatest light you'd see?

I believe I'd see the greatest light of the world. I believe I'd not just see the light that He spoke into being, but the Word of life and light Himself. Really think about that for a minute. When Adam was created he was already a man, he didn't come from the womb of a mother. He became from God's Word. In Genesis 1:26 (NKJV) "*Then God said*, "Let Us make man in Our image. In Genesis 2:7 (NKJV) "And the Lord God formed man of the dust of the ground, and breathed into his nostrils the breath of life; and man became a living being."

According to Genesis 2:15 (NKJV) "Then the LORD God took the man and put him in the garden of Eden to tend and keep it.

Now really imagine that you are Adam here. You are just created out of the dust of the ground and put in a garden. Is anyone else around here? There is One around. God spoke to Adam, and surely Adam heard Him. God took Adam and put him in the garden of Eden. Adam didn't just go there on his own, but he was taken there. Took is the past tense of take, which means to carry or transport something or somebody from one place to another. Adam was placed into his position, and God gave him a command to not eat of the tree of knowledge of good and evil Genesis 2:16–17.

And then God even brought every beast of the field and every bird of the air to Adam to see what he would call them Genesis 2:19. Adam gives names to all cattle, to all birds of the air, and to every beast of the field Genesis

2:20. Jesus is before all things, and before all creation, He was here before Adam the first man, He made Adam. We can see this truth in the first four words of the Holy Bible in Genesis chapter 1 it says: "In the beginning God." See Jesus is the image of the invisible God, the scripture says in Colossians 1:15-17 (NKJV) He is the image of the invisible God, the firstborn over all creation. For by Him all things were created that are in heaven and that are on earth, visible and invisible, whether thrones or dominions or principalities or powers. All things were created through Him and for Him, and He is before all things, and in Him all things consist.

John 1:1–3, Colossians 1:15–17, Genesis 1:1 all says that Jesus was in the beginning and before all things. See, Jesus was already in the beginning, and is the Beginning and He is also the End. He is the Word of God. His name is called The Word of God. Jesus is already the "Light and Life" that we need. He is the greatest Light.

> In Him was life, and the life was the light of men. And the light shines in the darkness, and the darkness did not comprehend it. (John 1:4–5, NKJV)

> This is the message which we have heard from Him and declare to you, that God is light and in Him is no darkness at all. (1 John 1:5, NKJV)

> He is the image of the invisible God, the firstborn over all creation. For by Him all things were created that are in heaven and that are on the earth, visible and invisible, whether thrones or dominions or principalities or powers. All thing were created through Him and for Him. And He is before all

things, and in Him all things consist. (Colossians 1:15–17, NKJV)

He was clothed with a robe dipped in blood, and His name is called The Word of God. (Revelation 19:13, NKJV)

"I am the Alpha and Omega, the Beginning and the End," says the Lord, "who is and who was and who is to come, the Almighty." (Revelation 1:8, NKJV)

———

The Image of the Man of the Dust, the Image of the Heavenly Man

And God said, Let us make man in our image, after our likeness: and let them have dominion over the fish of the sea, and over the fowl of the air, and over the cattle, and over all the earth, over every creeping thing that creepeth upon the earth. So God created man in His own image, in the image of God created he him, male and female created he them. (Genesis 1:26–27, KJV)

Jesus is the image of the invisible God, and we know that He was the firstborn over all creation. When I think about mankind made in the image of God, I factor in God's plan for mankind. I'm reminded of the Church that is called the body of Christ. Born-again Christians together make up the Body of Christ, the Bible calls us The Bride of Christ, Christ being the Bridegroom. What a plan God has made us in His image that connects us to Him as one.

Just as the three are one, so when we join with Him we are one with Him also. The prayer Jesus prayed to the Father before He suffered for all mankind was that we who were called would be one just as they are One. God wants' to join us to Himself, and make us one with Him.

> "That they all may be *one*, as *You, Father, are in Me, and I in You*; that they may be *one* in Us, that the world may believe that You sent Me. "And the glory which You gave Me I have given them, that they may be *one* just as *We are one*: *"I in them*, and *You in Me*; that they may be made perfect in *one*, and that the world may know that You have sent Me, and have loved them as You have loved Me. "And I have declared to them Your name, and will declare it, that the love with which You loved Me may be in them, and *I in them*." (John 17:21–23, 26, NKJV)

In 1 Corinthians 15:49 it says; "And as we have borne the image of the man of the dust,"

Who is the man of the dust? Adam. What image was this? In Genesis 1:26–27, God created man in His image and after His likeness, so what happened to Adams image? Romans 5:12 and 14, tells us that through one man sin entered the world. And Genesis 3:22 tells us, the man has become to know good and evil. We all have sinned and fallen short of the glory of God.

> Therefore, just as through one man sin entered the world, and death through sin, and thus death spread to all men, because all sinned—Nevertheless death reigned from Adam to Moses, even over those who had not sinned according to the likeness of the

transgression of Adam, who is a type of Him who was to come. (Romans 5:12, 14, NKJV)

The first man was of the earth, made of dust; the second Man is the Lord from heaven. As was the man of the dust, so also are those who are made of the dust; and as is the heavenly Man, so also are those who are heavenly. And as we have borne the image of the man of the dust, we shall also bear the image of the heavenly Man. (1 Corinthians 15:47–49, NKJV)

for all have sinned and fall short of the glory of God. (Romans 3:23, NKJV)

And the Lord God said, "The man has now become like one of us, knowing good and evil. He must not be allowed to reach out his hand and take also from the tree of life and eat, and live forever." (Genesis 3:22 NIV)

When Adam and Eve disobeyed God, their eyes were opened, and the world they viewed was not the same to them anymore; they would now know good and evil.

Then the eyes of both of them were opened, and they realized they were naked; So they sewed fig leaves together and made coverings for themselves. (Genesis 3:7, NIV)

Then the Lord God said, "Behold, the man has become like one of Us, to know good and evil. And now, lest he put out his hand and take also of the tree of life, and eat, and live forever-" (Genesis 3:22, NKJV)

Adam and Eve were naked when they were created, and this was fine, they were not ashamed since they were pure, but because they disobeyed God's word when God told Adam not to eat of the tree of knowledge of good and evil, they were ashamed and wanted to cover-up themselves from their sin, so they tried to do this by sowing fig leaves together. This is what sin felt like to them, to cover themselves from God. God then clothed Adam and Eve Himself with garments of animal skin.

> And they were both naked, the man and his wife, and were not ashamed.
>
> (Genesis 2:25, NKJV)

> The Lord God made garments of skin for Adam and his wife and clothed them.
>
> (Genesis 3:21, NIV)

Adam and Eve took their eyes off the Word of God, which were the words that God spoke to Adam to not eat of the tree of knowledge of good and evil. And we know they placed their eyes on their own desires instead.

> And the Lord God commanded the man, saying, "Of every tree of the garden you may freely eat; "but of the tree of knowledge of good and evil, you shall not eat, for in the day that you eat of it you shall surely die." (Genesis 2:16–17, NKJV)

> And when the woman saw that the tree was good for food, and that it was pleasant to the eyes, and a tree to be desired to make one wise, she took of

the fruit therof, and did eat, and gave also unto her husband with her, and he did eat. (Genesis 3:6, KJV)

———◦◦◦◦◦◦◦◦◦———

God Protected All Mankind

God loved Adam and Eve, His first created people, and He did protect them, and not only them, but all mankind! If you notice in Genesis 3:22, God did not want Adam and Eve to also eat from the tree of life and live forever. Why? Adam and Eve could have eaten from this tree instead of the tree of knowledge of good and evil. God only commanded them not to eat of one tree, which was the tree of knowledge of good and evil. If Adam and Eve would have eaten from the tree of life instead of the tree of knowledge of good and evil, don't you suppose that they would have lived forever in the light and goodness? Adam and Eve made a bad choice when they didn't obey the voice of God. God protected them by sending them out of the Garden of Eden, and He did not allow them to enter it. God also had the tree of life guarded. Just think, if they were to eat from the tree of life at that point when they sinned, they would be forever in sin and darkness.

> Then the Lord God said, "Behold the man has now become like one of Us, to know good and evil. And now, lest he put out his hand and take also from the tree of life, and eat and live forever"- therefore the Lord God sent him out of the garden of Eden to till the ground from which he was taken. So He drove out the man; and He placed cherubim at the east of the garden of Eden, and a flaming sword which

turned every way, to guard the way to the tree of life. (Genesis 3:22–24, NKJV)

We can learn from Adam and Eve's mistake and keep our eyes planted in the Word of God. The Lord wants us to keep our eyes focused on Him so that we would be a people full of the light of life (Jesus Christ). The lamp of the body is the eye!

> "No one, when he has lit a lamp, puts it in a secret place or under a basket, but on a lamp stand, that those who come in may see the light. "The lamp of the body is the eye. Therefore, when your eye is good, your whole body will be full of light. But when your eye is bad, your whole body also is full of darkness. Therefore take heed that the light which is in you is not darkness. "If then your whole body is full of light, having no part dark, the whole body will be full of light, as when the bright shining of a lamp gives you light." (Luke 11:33–36, NKJV)

> In Him was life, and the life was the light of men. (John 1:4, NKJV)

> This is the message which we have heard from Him and declare to you, that God is light and in Him is no darkness at all. (1 John 1:5, NKJV)

Our eye has to be good for our whole body to be full of light, and in Jesus there is no darkness at all. He is the light! Let's keep our eyes fixed on Him and be as a bright shining lamp! And just as God put Adam in the garden of Eden when He made him and gave him a command, and his choices, God also knew where He would put us when

He made us, and He gave us a command also and tells us what the bad choice is and the consequence of it. He also tells us what the good choice is and its reward.

We know the voice of God, and we also know the voice of the serpent. Today the choice remains the same for us—to eat from the tree of life that comes through Jesus Christ that is good, or partake of death and evil. He commands us to choose life and goodness, and walk in His ways.

> "See, I have set before you today life and good, death and evil, "in that I command you today to love the Lord your God, to walk in His ways, and to keep His commandments, His statutes, and His judgments, that you may live and multiply; and the Lord your God will bless you in the land which you go to possess.
>
> "I call heaven and earth as witnesses today against you, that I have set before you life and death, blessing and cursing; therefore choose life, that both you and your descendants may live; "that you may love the Lord your God, that you may obey His voice, and that you may cling to Him, for He is your life and the length of your days; and that you may dwell in the land which the LORD swore to your fathers, to Abraham, Isaac, and Jacob, to give them." (Deuteronomy 30:15–16, 19–20, NKJV)
>
> "The Lord will establish you as a holy people to Himself, just as He has sworn to you, if you keep the commandments of the Lord your God and walk in His ways. (Deuteronomy 28:9, NKJV)

When are you established as holy people to Him? If you *keep the commandments of the Lord your God and walk in His ways.* God wants us to make the choice to have life and love Him just as He loves us. He could have given us no choice at all. Let's think about that. Let's say God didn't give us a choice in the matter. Do you wonder how God could even really feel like we love Him? God wants to be loved. He made us to be drawn to Him and seek Him.

He's our Creator. Think about it. The Creator created you. He breathed life into you when you were born. He watched you grow and taught you along the way. Now He's looking at you and sees what a masterpiece you are in His eyes. He loves you with all that He is, and He's awaiting your response to Him. Are you going to respond to the One who made you? Is your response going to be love? That's what He's looking for. He's looking for His creation to love Him back with all of our heart, soul, mind, and strength.

He gave you a choice, life, and blessing, or death and cursing. He even gave you a way to walk in this life. He gave His own life as an example to follow Him. Think if you were the creator, you made all things, even the people in the world. Wouldn't you want to be loved back by them? How would you be able to feel loved back by them of their choice? Certainly they would have a choice, and you'd set the path for them to follow it along the way, and you'd teach them how to walk down the path of life, and you'd expect them to choose you who created them in love.

You'd even command them to love you, you'd make it the first command. God has feelings also, and the greatest one of all is love. He gives us love and most definitely expects it back in return. What's the first and great commandment of all?

Jesus said to him, "You shall love the Lord your God with all your heart, with all your soul, and with all your mind.' "This is the first and great commandment. (Matthew 22:37–38, NKJV)

And then what happens? He blesses you, and you live and multiply.

———ᴡᴡ∘ᴄᴇᴛᴏ◉ᴛᴇᴅ∘ᴡᴡ———

Jesus Restores!

Just like in the natural world, God spoke the light into being upon the world necessary for life. He also had a plan for the Word (Jesus) to be born into the world to be revealed to us as an everlasting light that gives everlasting life. Notice the words, *everlasting light* and *life*?

Jesus was always the light in the beginning before creation, and He came to us all as the true light to a world in darkness. Jesus came as the light to become our Savior that we should not abide in darkness! This is the light that God gave to us that was the true light.

"I have come as a light into the world, that whoever believes in Me should not abide in darkness. (John 12:46, NKJV)

That was the true Light which gives light to every man coming into the world. (John 1:9)

In Him was life, and the life was the light of men. (John 1:4, NKJV)

Now the natural light became because God spoke. The true light, the greatest light (God's Son, Jesus) came into the world by the word of God spoken. Jesus was spoken about in the Old Testament by the holy priests and prophets who were given the inspiration of the word of God to speak. These priests and prophets foretold that Jesus, the Son of God, would be born into the world. One of them that spoke about Jesus to come was the prophet Isaiah.

> "And she will bring forth a Son, and you shall call His name JESUS, for He will save His people from their sins." So all this was done that it might be fulfilled which was spoken by the Lord through the prophet, saying: "Behold, the virgin shall be with child, and bear a Son, and they shall call His name Immanuel," which is translated, "God with us." (Matthew 1:21–23, NKJV)

> "Therefore the Lord Himself will give you a sign: Behold, the virgin shall conceive and bear a Son, and shall call His name Immanuel. (Isaiah 7:14, NKJV)

> For unto us a Child is born, Unto us a Son is given; And the government will be upon His shoulder. And His name will be called Wonderful, Counselor, Mighty God, Everlasting Father, Prince of Peace. Of the increase of His government and peace there will be no end, Upon the throne of David and over His kingdom, To order it and establish it with judgment and justice from that time forward, even forever. The zeal of the Lord of hosts will perform this. (Isaiah 9:6–7, NKJV)

And we also know that the prophet Isaiah foretold that Jesus would be a "great light," And the scripture says that it's the people who walked in darkness that see Him as a great light. We all know what it's like to walk in darkness. If you can't remember then turn off all the lights around you at night and try to walk around for a while. You'll find it's hard to see anything or where you're going and headed. You'll probably feel alone—scared even. We all walked in darkness because of sin in our lives. It's no fun to walk in the night and be full of darkness.

We've all fallen short of the glory of God. We know the experience, but light has dawned!

The people who walked in darkness Have seen a great light; Those who dwelt in the land of the shadow of death, Upon them a light has shined. (Isaiah 9:2, NKJV)

The fulfilling of Isaiah 9:2 is talked about in Matthew 4:16.

The people who sat in darkness have seen a great light, And upon those who sat in the region and shadow of death Light has dawned." (Matthew 4:16, NKJV)

Are you sitting in darkness? Are you walking in the night? You don't have to anymore because Light has dawned upon you!

Indeed He says, "It is too small a thing that You should be My Servant To raise up the tribes of Jacob, and to restore the preserved ones of Israel; I will also give You as a light to the Gentiles, That You should be My salvation to the ends of the earth.'" (Isaiah 49:6, NKJV)

God gave Jesus Christ as a light to all of us and to be God's Salvation to the ends of the earth. See, Jesus was already in the beginning, He was the Word, He was the Light, and He came to earth for the Father's purposes.

"For I have come down from heaven, not to do My own will, but the will of Him who sent Me. "This is the will of the Father who sent Me, that of all that He has given Me I should lose nothing, but should raise it up at the last day. "And this is the will of Him who sent Me, that everyone who sees the Son and believes in Him may have everlasting life; and I will raise him up at the last day." (John 6:38–40, NKJV)

We can clearly see that Jesus is the Word of God; His name is called The Word of God and we know the Word is the Son. The Word became flesh when He was born into the world.

And the Word became flesh and dwelt among us, and we beheld His glory, the glory as of the only begotten of the Father, full of grace and truth. (John 1:14, NKJV)

He was clothed with a robe dipped in blood, and His name is called The Word of God. (Revelations 19:13, NKJV)

Jesus Christ was always a light, but He became a light to the world as our Savior! And remember, in Luke 2:30–32, Simeon says, "For my eyes have seen *Your Salvation* which You have prepared before the face of *all peoples, A light to bring revelation* to the Gentiles, and the glory of Your people Israel." And in John 12:46 (NKJV) Jesus says, "I have come as a light into the world, that whoever believes in Me should not abide in darkness. And

John 1:9 says that Jesus is the true Light, which gives light to every man coming into the world. That means to every man, all of us. That also includes Adam and Eve from the beginning; He was the true light and greatest light to them as He is to us now. Jesus is the true light that gave Himself to us, to be the true Light in us. Jesus was always the light in the beginning before creation, and He came to us all as the light. And we know this is the greatest light that God gave to us that is the true light of the world.

> Then Jesus spoke to them again, saying, "I am the light of the world. He who follows Me shall not walk in darkness, but have the light of life." (John 8:12, NKJV)

Jesus restored mankind's relationship back to the Father, and He is our entrance into the relationship with the Father and to everlasting life.

> Jesus said to him, "I am the way, the truth, and the life.' No one comes to the Father except through Me. (John 14:6, NKJV)

> So that sin reigned in death, even so grace might reign through righteousness to eternal life through Jesus Christ our Lord. (Romans 5:21, NKJV)

God loved mankind so much that He wanted to send His only Son to us.

> "For God so loved the world that He gave His only begotten Son, that whoever believes in Him should not perish but have everlasting life. "For God did not send His Son into the world to condemn the world, but that the world through Him might be saved. (John 3:16–17, NKJV)

Wow! Surely God loves us so much that He did not send Jesus Christ to come into the world to condemn the world. We know the world was in sin, and He came to save. He sure came to save the day! He came with love, and love came with Him! We can clearly see that Jesus is the true light needed to a world in darkness. I mentioned how we bore the image of the man of the dust (Adam). 1 Corinthians 15:49, NKJV continues with, "We shall also bear the image of the heavenly Man. God originally gave mankind a heavenly image (His Image). We are able to bear the image of the Heavenly Man (Jesus Christ) when we are born again. Now through Jesus Christ, God's Son, the heavenly image is restored back to us.

We can only bear this heavenly image when we are birthed into it. "And as we have borne the image of the man of the dust, we shall also bear the image of the heavenly Man." (1 Corinthians 15:49, NKJV)

In Genesis 1, we see how the words "and God said," are completed with "and it was so," speaking about all God's creation coming into existence, the Earth *became* a place where all God's plans would *become* all that He said it would be. Let's not forget Ephesians 5:27, NKJV

> That He might present her to Himself a glorious church, not having spot or wrinkle or any such thing, but that she should be holy and without blemish. (Ephesians 5:27, NKJV)

Jesus Christ is returning for a glorious church without spot or wrinkle, which tells us a lot! It tells us what He planned, *when we became, we will become*! "Glorious!" We *became* His chosen people to *become* His church, His glorious church! When God had us in mind, God knew the exact process He would have us go through to become the glorious church He sees in the end; just like the caterpillar, God has been building His church for about 2,000 years now. Something to think about when you look at the sunrise every morning—God's Son, Jesus Christ, is the greatest light of the world, and the greatest light in your life, brighter than the sun are His glorious plans for your life! Don't doubt that!

2

A New Life to Begin

> I will bring the blind by the way they did not know;
> I will lead them in paths they have not known. I
> will make darkness light before them, And crooked
> places straight. These things I will do for them, And
> not forsake them. (Isaiah 42:16, NKJV)

Life is the start of something new to begin. Life is the
beginning of an end.

Jesus Came to Change Us!

In the natural world we are always going through new
processes due to a changing world, and it's always by the
end of something to the beginning of the new. We can
see this clearly throughout history, the end of one thing
and the beginning of the new thing. We must understand
that as the times change, we have to change with it. When

we don't change with the time, the time still changes, but we won't. This will cause us to live a past-tense life in a present-tense world around us.

If we never move with what's going on around us then there will never be the start of anything new to begin in our lives. Isn't that a profound fact? See, we need to understand that about 2,000 years ago God sent His Son into the world to change the world. Jesus came to change us! He knows what process He will have you go through to become that butterfly that He sees in the end. Your life process may be much different than someone else's because He is shaping you into what He's called you to individually be because we all have an individual purpose to fulfill.

And although our life process may be different, the path to righteousness remains the same! He is our Deliverer who came to deliver us from our sins and restore our relationship back to the Father. It's time for the world to stop living a past-tense life! If we don't go onto our new life to begin in us, then we will be corrupt till the end. The end of the old life is the beginning of the new life.

We have to let go of the corrupt one and let it end before the new life can begin in us. Isn't that profound? Jesus Christ gave Himself to us, the true light and greatest light, for us all to see. The world doesn't have to walk in darkness because the Light has come to us. The light shines in the darkness—the darkness is the world, but we must see that the light shines even in our dark world.

Jesus Christ did come to change the world, it's time to begin a new life and walk in the light and life of His Word and honor the Son and give glory to God.

"That all should honor the Son just as they honor the Father. He who does not honor the Son does not honor the Father who sent Him. "Most assuredly, I say to you, he who hears My words and believes in Him who sent Me has everlasting life, and shall not come into judgment, but has passed from death into life. (John 5:23–24, NKJV)

Life knows its home. It's seen the light and finds rest in God alone.

Many people have said, "Light is at the end of the tunnel." We must know that the light is at the door, and it's here and now. Don't wait to get to the end of the tunnel to see the light, open your eyes and see the door of Light here and now! See, there's a door for us to enter where we can follow the light to the door, see the light at the door and knock at the door. We need to be knocking at the door, if we want to enter into the light of life. Jesus is the light; Jesus is the door for us to enter.

We have to enter by the door of light to enter into the light and find life.

> "Most assuredly, I say to you, he who does not enter the sheepfold by the door, but climbs up some other way, the same is a thief and a robber. (John 10:1, NKJV)

See, there is no other way to enter into the "Light of Life," but by the door. Jesus is the way the truth and the life.

> Jesus said to him, "I am the way, the truth, and the life, No one comes to the Father except through Me. (John 14:6, NKJV)

Then Jesus said to them again, "Most assuredly, I say to you, I am the door of the sheep. (John 10:7, NKJV)

"I am the door, If anyone enters by Me, he will be saved, and will go in and out and find pasture. (John 10:9, NKJV)

In Him was life, and the life was the light of men. (John 1:4, NKJV)

We must know that the Light is here and now for us, and we don't have to wait till the end of the tunnel to see it.

———————

Breaking Out of the Tunnel

That You may say to the prisoners, 'Go forth,' To those who are in darkness, 'Show yourselves.' (Isaiah 49:9, NKJV)

Our life can be a tunnel—a tunnel of enclosed darkness. We don't have to go through life helpless and hopeless. Nobody needs to be walking in darkness dead, trying to find rest, waiting to get to the light. It's time to break out of the tunnel, see the light at the door, and start knocking!

Jesus said to her, "I am the resurrection and the life. He who believes in Me, though he may die, he shall live. "And whoever lives and believes in Me shall never die. Do you believe this?" (John 11:25–26, NKJV)

"Ask, and it will be given to you; seek, and you will find; knock, and it will be opened to you. "For to everyone who asks receives, and he who seeks finds, and to him who knocks it will be opened. (Matthew 7:7–8, NKJV)

Therefore He says: " Awake, you who sleep. Arise from the dead. And Christ will give you light." (Ephesians 5:14, NKJV)

It's Resurrection Day!

See, we can rest now in Jesus Christ and live. We can reach home through Jesus Christ. We can rest in the Lord by trusting Him with our lives, when we trust Him with our lives, we believe that He both speaks with His own mouth and fulfills it with His own hand. We believe that He's put us where He wants us, and we obey His commands. We believe we will overcome the world with our faith believing that Jesus is the Son of God.

We believe that it's the Lord's purpose that prevails! We live according to His own will and His own ways, and we stop living according to our will and our ways because many are the plans in our heart. Let go of your many plans and follow after His! He knows the plans He has for you, and they are good plans, plans to prosper you and not to harm you. God has called you to become what He has said.

Let Him rule in your heart and take over your life then you will be able to walk in all of God's purposes for your life. He wants your heart—all of it! See, it's when He takes over. Take over our lives Jesus, take over! Less of our ways and more of His. Just step back and surrender, rest and let Him prevail!

> For whatever is born of God overcomes the world. And this is the victory that has overcome the world-our faith. Who is he who overcomes the world, but he who believes that Jesus is the Son of God? (1 John 5:4–5, NKJV)

> Many are the plans in a person's heart, but it is the LORD's purpose that prevails. (Proverbs 19:21, NIV)

Where are we going in this world if we walk by it? We cannot be a part of the world and also a part of heaven. We can't be divided, or we will fall. Light has no part in darkness. Remember God saw that the light was good, and He did separate it from the darkness. We are of the day; we are divided from the darkness, walk in the day! We are sons of the light and sons of the day!

> "If a kingdom is divided against itself, that kingdom cannot stand. (Mark 3:24, NKJV)

> And God saw the light, that it was good; and God divided the light from the darkness. (Genesis 1:4, NKJV)

> You are all sons of the light and sons of the day. We are not of the night nor of darkness. (1 Thessalonians 5:5, NKJV)

We must choose one or the other, either the world and all of its lusts, or the God of heaven and earth (Jesus Christ). I choose Jesus, who first chose me! My prayer is that you do too! Don't become a part of the fading world and all the lusts of it, surely it will pass away. Heaven has a higher calling for us. Choose Jesus who first chose you. Walk in His ways and fulfill the Father's plan in love for the Father and the world that He's spoken.

Surely then we'll have treasures in heaven that will not compare to the treasures of this world. The earth and its treasures will surely pass away, and we don't want to be a people that just pass away, but pass on. We want to pass onto our home in heaven with the Father who created us in love!

> And the world is passing away, and the lust of it; but he who does the will of God abides forever. (1 John 2:17, NKJV)

> "Do not lay up for yourselves treasures on earth, where moth and rust destroy and where thieves break in and steal; "but lay up for yourselves treasures in heaven, where neither moth nor rust destroys and where thieves do not break in and steal. "For where your treasure is, there your heart will be also. (Matthew 6:19–21, NKJV)

We don't want to pass away with the world; we want to pass on away from the world to our home with the Father in heaven. I don't like to see it, but surely there are people who are just waiting for their time in this life to pass away. No. press on, and when your time comes you'll pass on! Head towards the goal, for your prize is in heaven. We're not just mere nobodies, we're purposely somebody's! And we are purposed to the Father.

You might want to give up on yourself; people might want to give up on you, but He sure will never give up on you! He knows the plans He has for you, and He knows what you shall become! We're not created to pass away. We're meant to pass onto a higher place where we are eternally destined. It's a place that will never pass away, but a place of eternal existence with the Father.

Life is a circle with an inner center. Inside the circle is a light for all to enter.

> Let your eyes look straight ahead, And your eyelids look right before you. (Proverbs 4:25, NKJV)

Our world is one big gigantic circle. We all live in it. People have said, "It is the circle of life." On a physical aspect, we are living in the world. We know scientists can go out of the world at which we live and explore beyond our planet. The world thinks this is an amazing accomplishment for man, but let's not forget that there's only one true way out of this world that only one man accomplished for all mankind (The Man Christ Jesus!).

Jesus came to give us an entrance into the kingdom of God, which is not of this world. We can't get into God's kingdom unless we go through Jesus Christ who made it possible for all to enter into it.

> Jesus answered, "My kingdom is not of this world. If My kingdom were of this world, My servant would fight, so that I should not be delivered to the Jews; but now My kingdom is not from here." (John 18:36, NKJV)

> Jesus said to him, "I am the way, the truth, and the life, No one comes to the Father except through Me. (John 14:6, NKJV)

Jesus is the inner center of the circle of life. We can see His light, and follow it into the center where He is, and He is the way to enter into the inner circle, because He is the door. On earth we can see everything around us well because everything is visible to us. When we were born into the world and opened our eyes for the first time, we seen the light in the world. This is also true when we are born again in order for us to see the kingdom of God.

Our eyes are then opened up to a new life that's full of light. We will then be able to see the kingdom of God with our spiritual senses so to speak.

> Jesus answered and said to him, "Most assuredly, I say to you, unless one is born again, he cannot see the kingdom of God." Nicodemus said to Him, "How can a man be born when he is old? Can he enter a second time into his mother's womb and be born?" Jesus answered. "Most assuredly, I say to you, unless one is born of water and the Spirit, he cannot enter the kingdom of God. "That which is born of the flesh is flesh, and that which is born of the Spirit is spirit. "Do not marvel that I said to you, 'You must be born again.' (John 3:3–7, NKJV)

> The Jesus called a little child to Him, set him in the midst of them, and said, "Assuredly, I say to you, unless you are converted and become as little children, you will by no means enter the kingdom of heaven. (Matthew 18:2–3, NKJV)

So there's a circle of life in which we live that is our planet, the world, but also an inner center where there is the Light of Life, Jesus, shining in the center for us to see. Jesus is the door where the light comes.

"I am the door, If anyone enters by Me, he will be saved, and will go in and out and find pasture. (John 10:9, NKJV)

We have to follow the light into the center of the circle of everlasting life where He is, to have real life.

> "As long as I am in the world, I am the light of the world." (John 9:5, NKJV)

> Then Jesus spoke to them again, saying, "I am the light of the world, He who follows Me shall not walk in darkness, but have the light of life." (John 8:12, NKJV)

> Jesus is the way, the truth, and the life!
> Jesus said to him, "I am the way, the truth, and the life, No one comes to the Father except through Me. (John 14:6, NKJV)

People can go around the center of the circle of everlasting light and life where Jesus is and never enter into it. People can keep wondering around in a world that is full of darkness and have no peace. People can stop walking in circles around the world and pause for a moment, and see the light that comes from the door (the center) where Jesus is, and we all can truly have life and peace forever.

> Then Jesus spoke to them again, saying, "I am the light of the world. He who follows Me shall not walk in darkness, but have the light of life." (John 8:12, NKJV)

The sun cannot always shine upon us, and it could never shine in us, but Jesus the Son of God can. He can not only shine upon us always, but gives light to every man as it says in John 1:9. Whenever someone gives us something and we receive it, it's ours to keep forever if we want to. The same is true about Jesus, He gives Himself to us for us to receive Him, and when we receive Him, He wants us to keep Him forever. Jesus is the light prepared for the Father's purposes, and when we receive Him, we receive the true light and greatest light, the light that we need.

We can see that the light originated from the Word (Jesus) because the Word (Jesus) is the light. So the Word is able to give light to us as it says in John 1:9. Evolution has these technical explanations for the creation of the light. Listen. It's very simple; "the Light created the light, and is the light." Or you can say, "The Light of heaven and earth created the light upon the earth and is the light in the earth." It's as simple as that! It's called *God's Word*, Jesus the Creator.

Listen there is no sun god! There is only the Son of God! Jesus is the light we worship, because Jesus is the light. The light of the world is the light in the world! He is before the day was!

> "Therefore know this day, and consider it in your heart, that the LORD Himself is God in heaven above and on the earth beneath; there is no other. (Deuteronomy 4:39, NKJV)
>
> I, even I, am the LORD, and besides Me there is no savior. Indeed before the day was, I am He; And there is no one who can deliver out of My hand; I work, and who will reverse it?" (Isaiah 43:11, 13, NKJV)

The next scripture tells us also that Jesus is the beginning and the end. He is past, present, and future.

> "I am the Alpha and the Omega, the Beginning and the End," says the Lord, "who is and who was and who is to come, the Almighty." (Revelation 1:8, NKJV)

> "Look to Me, and be saved, all you ends of the earth! For I am God, and there is no other. (Isaiah 45:22, NKJV)

Jesus came and restored to us! He did this by saving us from our sins when He laid down His own life for us all in love. The image of the Heavenly Man (Jesus Christ) is the image we bear when we are born again. Jesus restored this image back to us so that we can now be a loving and holy people unto the Lord—worshiping a loving and Holy God now and forever. We are full of the Light of Life when we are born again.

He gives His own Spirit to us, the Light gives light to us, He gives eternal life to us in Him and with Him, and He gives His love to us. When a person is born again, they might not be able to see any change in themselves as they look at themselves in a mirror let's say. But to God, He sees us in His image. He sees His Spirit in us, His Life in us, His Light in us, and His Love in us. We have Jesus Christ that we received into our lives who is the Light and Life, and He has given us Himself the true Light and eternal life through Him.

And we have His love abiding in us, as He's in us. In God's eyes when He looks at us, He sees His image, and indeed He likes it. We become one with Him!

"that they may be one, as You, Father, are in Me, and I in You; that they also may be one in Us, that the world may believe that You sent Me. (John 17:21, NKJV)

"I in them, and You in Me; that they may be made perfect in one, and that the world may believe that You sent Me, and I have loved them as You have loved Me. (John 17:23, NKJV)

But now in Christ Jesus you who were far off have been brought near by the blood of Christ. For He Himself is our peace, who has made both one, and has broken down the middle wall of separation. Now, therefore, you are no longer strangers and foreigners, but fellow citizens with the saints and members of the household of God, having been built on the foundation of the apostles and prophets, Jesus Christ Himself being the chief cornerstone, in whom the whole building, being fitted together, grows into a holy temple in the Lord, in whom you also are being built together for a dwelling place of God in the Spirit. (Ephesians 2:13–14, 19–22, NKJV)

God's people are restored back to Him through Jesus Christ the Word. God does not look at His people and see a corrupted person. We have to identify ourselves in God who made us new. The change is made first on the inside, and as we begin to walk in the inward change, the Spirit transforms us.

We as the church, the people of God, begin inside, and then we go outside. We make a difference in this world when we walk in it with fruit to give out to hungry people. It's about walking in all the fruit of the Spirit of love, joy, peace, longsuffering, kindness, goodness, faithfulness, gentleness, and self-control. The Spirit, manifesting all of its fruits—This is what people are hungry for in the world. When we begin walking in the Spirit, the fruit is visible on the outside of us. It's visible in our actions, character, and emotions. It's in our hands, in serving and giving, and praising and worshipping. We're able to give His fruit to others, He who's in us, is giving. He is a God who gives Himself to all.

Life is seeing the starting line and shining to the finishing line.

God has a starting line for our lives. Jesus Christ is the way! And God has a finishing line for our lives and already sees where the finishing line is, even though we can't yet. Imagine yourself at the starting line; this is where you first give your life to Christ. The whistle blows and you started the race, your intentions are to take off and run. After all, you are excited. You are ready to be a winner, but you first must begin by walking because every lap you make, you begin to transform. The process is delicate because you are going to become that butterfly. You will learn to endure along the way being able to bear prolonged exertion, pain, or hardships, it is a strenuous effort that requires your physical effort, energy, strength, and you will learn to be able to tolerate suffering and have the ability to survive, having persistence despite the ravage of times.

And in it all, while you delicately remain obedient your fruit will begin to ripen for the harvest. And the more laps you make, the more transformed you'll become. Your fruit will slowly ripen, now you start to run the race. These laps are your life. You can't see the finish line, yet the race is not over, so keep going. Whether you have just begun your race by walking, or it's time for you to start running, just keep going! The finish line is ahead!

> Or do you not know that your body is the temple of the Holy Spirit who is in you, whom you have from God, and you are not your own? For you were bought at a price; therefore glorify God in your body and in your spirit, which are God's. (1 Corinthians 6:19–20, NKJV)

> But the fruit of the Spirit is love, joy, peace, longsuffering, kindness, goodness, faithfulness, gentleness, self-control. Against such there is no law. And those who are Christ's have crucified the flesh with its passions and desires. If we live in the Spirit, let us also walk in the Spirit. (Galatians 5:22–25, NKJV)

Jesus finished His race on earth. He shined His way to the finish line, and He is the shining finish line. He's the beginning and the end. He's the Starting line and the Finishing line! When we get to the finishing line we can say like Jesus did, I have finished the work, which You have given me to do. And also be like Paul and say, I have finished the race:

> "I have glorified You on the earth. I have finished the work which You have given Me to do. (John 17:4)

> I have fought the good fight, I have finished the race, I have kept the faith. (2 Timothy 4:7–8, NKJV)

> Therefore we also, since we are surrounded by so great a cloud of witnesses, let us lay aside every

weight, and the sin which so easily ensnares us, and let us run with endurance the race that is set before us, looking unto Jesus the author and finisher of our faith, who for the joy that was set before Him endured the cross, despising the shame, and has sat down at the right hand of the throne of God. (Hebrews 12:1–2, NKJV)

Jesus fulfilled His Father's plan. He raised Himself back from the dead on the third day, and He is alive today!

"He is not here, but is risen! Remember how He spoke to you when He was still in Galilee, "saying, 'The Son of Man must be delivered into the hands of sinful men, and be crucified, and the third day rise again.'" (Luke 24:6–7, NKJV)

Then He said to them, "Thus it is written, and thus it was necessary for the Christ to suffer and to rise from the dead the third day, "and that repentance and remission of sins should be preached in His name to all nations, beginning at Jerusalem. (Luke 24:46–47, NKJV)

In Luke 24:46–47, Jesus spoke to His disciples after He died and rose from the dead on the third day. Jesus died for mankind because He loved His Father and all of mankind.

"But that the world may know that I love the Father, and as the Father gave Me commandment, so I do. Arise, let us go from here. (John 14:31, NKJV)

By this we know love, because He laid down His life for us. And we also ought to lay down our lives for the brethren. (1 John 3:16, NKJV)

Jesus *reconciled* us back to the Father. This word literally means to bring two or more people back into a friendly relationship with each other after a dispute, returning to a friendly relationship. Jesus Christ *returned* us to a friendly relationship with God. This word means to come or go back to a place after leaving it, or come or go back to a former condition.

> Now all things are of God, who has reconciled us to Himself through Jesus Christ, and has given us the ministry of reconciliation, that is, that God was in Christ reconciling the world to Himself, not imputing their trespasses to them, and has committed to us the word of reconciliation. (2 Corinthians 5:18–19, NKJV)

> But now in Christ Jesus you who were far off have been brought near by the blood of Christ. For He Himself is our peace, who has made us both one, and has broken down the middle wall of separation, (Ephesians 2:13–14, NKJV)

We are not here to do our own will, but only the will of God who sent us here also. God sent His only Son to us to be born into the world to save mankind from their sins, and through Jesus Christ we are saved from our sins and restored back to God. *He has delivered us from the power of darkness!*

> But God demonstrated His own love toward us, in that while we were still sinners, Christ died for us. (Romans 5:8, NKJV)

> He has delivered us from the power of darkness and conveyed us into the kingdom of the Son of His love, in whom we have redemption through His

blood, the forgiveness of sins. (Colossians 1:13–14, NKJV)

Colossians 1:13 says Jesus *has delivered us* from the power of darkness. The world doesn't have to be in darkness anymore because *He has delivered us from it.* The Word of God (Jesus) actually left heaven and came to the earth through a virgin named Mary and was born as truly God and human.

"For I have come down from heaven, not to do My own will, but the will of Him who sent Me. (John 6:38, NKJV)

"Behold, the virgin shall be with child and bear a Son, and they shall call His name Immanuel," which is translated, "God with us." (Matthew 1:23, NKJV)

God became flesh and showed us that sin has no power over Him, and that He could overcome this world in perfection. Jesus is the perfect example of love. We too can be an example of the love of Jesus Christ with the help of the Holy Spirit in us. Jesus demonstrated to us with compassion, His own love for His Father and us so that we would know what He wants of us. *That is love for God and each other.*

Jesus said to him, "'You shall love the LORD your God with all your heart, with all your soul, and with all your mind. "This is the first and great commandment. "And the second is like it: 'You shall love your neighbor as yourself.' (Matthew 22:37–38, NKJV)

"This is My commandment, that you love one another as I have loved you. (John 15:12, NKJV)

God's love is like no other. His love never changes. He is love, and He never changes. Our love changes, we get angry with people and sometimes we love them and sometimes we don't, God gets angry too, but His love never changes! He wants us to love as He does. Now, we cannot overcome this life without Him. Jesus overcame this world, and we can too through Him. He took the punishment that we deserved. He bore all sins and iniquities for us on the cross. God actually died for us, and not only that, but willingly laid down His own life.

> For whatever is born of God overcomes the world. And this is the victory that has overcome the world-our faith. Who is he who overcomes the world, but he who believes that Jesus is the Son of God? (1 John 5:4–5, NKJV)

> "No one takes My life from Me, but I lay it down of Myself, I have power to lay it down and I have power to take it again. This command I have received from My Father." (John 10.18, NKJV)

Jesus showed us that death has no victory over Him. He arose from the dead on the third day and even walked on earth for forty days before He went back to His home with the Father in heaven.

> "knowing that Christ, having been raised from the dead, dies no more. Death no longer has dominion over Him. (Romans 6:9, NKJV)

"to whom He also presented Himself alive after His
suffering by many infallible proofs, being seen by
them during forty days and speaking of the things
pertaining to the kingdom of God. (Acts 1:3, NKJV)

We have to live by the example that Jesus Christ came
to show us, but we can only do that by His Holy Spirit
in us and walking in obedience to His Word, plans, and
purposes. God gave us a way to do this by giving us His
Spirit that is truth and life. God actually teaches us how to
live according to His will when we receive Him. This is so
that we can do according to His will.

> "But the Helper, the Holy Spirit, whom the Father
> will send in My name, He will teach you all things,
> and bring to your remembrance all things that I said
> to you. (John 14:26, NKJV)

> "However, when He, the Spirit of truth, has come,
> He will guide you into all truth; for He will not
> speak on His own authority, but whatever He hears
> He will speak; and He will tell you things to come.
> (John 16:13, NKJV)

> for it is God who works in you both to will and to
> do for His good pleasure. (Philippians 2:13, NKJV)

When we receive His Holy Spirit, God's Spirit actually
lives in our bodies. It's amazing to think about really, but
don't just stop at thinking about it. Get a revelation of Him
in you. If you received the Holy Spirit, take a look at your
own body and see yourself as you are, you don't need a mirror
to do this. Look at your hands, your feet. Now realize this,

you are not alone! Somewhere in you is someone greater than you. It's His Holy Spirit, you are not your own!

You are here for God's master plans and purposes. Don't be self-focused, be God focused. Include yourself in His plans and purposes for your life. How else are you going to fulfill them if you don't? Make it a part of your day to say, what do You want me to do for You today, Lord? Or what can I do to help someone today, Lord? We are serving people to serve God.

It's not all about just you anymore, it's about His plans and purposes, and He that's in you who is able to accomplish it all.

> Or do you not know that your body is the temple of the Holy Spirit who is in you, whom you have from God, and you are not your own? For you were bought at a price; therefore glorify God in your body and in your spirit, which are God's. (1 Corinthians 6:19–20, NKJV)

It's about recognizing that He's in you and realize that He is a part of your life now. Let Him help you make those decisions and choices. We can only do what we have the ability to do, but God does the impossible! And with God nothing is impossible! It's not that we are able, it's about Him that's in us who is able to do all things.

When you look at it this way, it's more than purely thinking. It's a revelation that you can look at your own physical body and know that He's somewhere in you too. God is so cool; tell Him how cool He is! Say Lord, ("use me for Your Kingdom, It's not about me!") We want to see the Kingdom of God and not only that, but enter into it, we have to be born again. If you haven't received Jesus Christ and been born of water and Spirit, *believe in your heart,* now is the time to *confess with your mouth the Lord Jesus, believe* that *Jesus is the Son of God, believe in your heart* that God *has* raised Him from the dead, *repent* of your sins, and *accept* Jesus' sacrificial death on the cross for your sins, and *receive Him into your life. Be water baptized in the name of the Lord Jesus Christ, and filled with the Holy Spirit* and *with fire.* He will guide you into all truth.

> That if you confess with your mouth the Lord Jesus and believe in your heart that God has raised Him from the dead, you will be saved. For with the heart one believes unto righteousness, and with the mouth confession is made unto salvation. For "whoever calls on the name of the LORD shall be saved." (Romans 10:9–10, 13, NKJV)

> "Repent therefore and be converted, that your sins may be blotted out, so that times of refreshing may come from the presence of the Lord, (Acts 3:19, NKJV)

> Then Peter said to them, "Repent and let everyone of you be baptized in the name of Jesus Christ for the remission of sins: and you shall receive the gift of the Holy Spirit. "For the promise is to you and to your children, and to all who are afar off, as many as the Lord our God will call." And with many other words he testified and exhorted them, saying, "Be saved from this perverse generation." Then those who gladly received his word were baptized, and that day about three thousand souls were added to them. (Acts 2:38–41, NKJV)

Jesus answered and said to him, "Most assuredly, I say to you, unless one is born again, he cannot see the kingdom of God." Nicodemus said to Him, "How can a man be born when he is old? Can he enter a second time into his mother's womb and be born?" Jesus answered, "Most assuredly, I say to you, unless one is born of water and the Spirit, he cannot enter the kingdom of God. "That which is born of the flesh is flesh, and that which is born of the Spirit is spirit. "Do not marvel that I said to you, 'You must be born again.' (John 3:3–7, NKJV)

"My sheep hear My voice, and I know them, and they follow Me. "And I give them eternal life, and they shall never perish; neither shall anyone snatch them out of My hand. (John 10:27–28, NKJV)

Walk the Talk

Get those feet walking for Him and get those hands helping for Him! Don't just talk about the talk, walk the talk. He is what the talk is about in the Holy Bible, and we have to walk about what was talked about. Jesus Christ is the Word of God, and in His own words and demonstration He has given us the revelation of Himself as He talked about it all and demonstrated it all. His name is called the Word of God, and we learn from His demonstration. We need His Word in our life. We need the Holy Bible!

We must know He did not just talk, He walked! He fulfilled His purpose! If Jesus Christ, the Word of God, came to walk in His own words, truly we must also. He was the Word walking in His words! We must walk in His words. We'll fulfill our purpose by following in the example that was talked about and walked about. We should want to be a people who are moving about His Word, this is our motivation. It's when we open up our heart to His Word and let the Word get into our heart.

We will be walking in His Word in the world. We must have faith to do it. We can't just be talking; we must be walking it too. If you've just reached the starting line, the whistle just blew for you. It's time to get those feet walking! See, Jesus did show mankind how He wants mankind to live, and He's given us Himself that we should know Him.

He's forgiven all our sins and bore all our grief. Jesus is the face of God's love for the world. it's His face that we seek because He is our true love, a love that never does end!

> He who does not love does not know God, for God is love. In this the love of God was manifested toward us, that God has sent His only begotten Son into the world, that we might live through Him. In this is love, not that we loved God, but that He loved us and sent His Son to be the propitiation for our sins. (1 John 4:8–10, NKJV)

> The Lord has appeared of old to me, saying: "Yes, I have loved you with an everlasting love; Therefore with lovingkindness I have drawn you. (Jeremiah 31:3, NKJV)

> Now may the God of peace who brought up our Lord Jesus Christ from the dead, that great Shepherd of the sheep, through the blood of the everlasting covenant, make you complete in every good work to do His will, working in you what is well pleasing in His sight, through Jesus Christ, to whom be glory forever and ever. Amen. (Hebrews 13:20–21, NKJV)

3

Eternal Peace, a Changing Life, and Our Helper

There Is No End to Jesus' Peace

Life is peace, knowing that He's there. Life knows that He will lift the burdens and share.

We live in a day when people need a lot of peace. We have to know that Jesus is always there for us. We have to receive His peace in our lives because truthfully, we need it. We aren't going to get through this life with the peace of the world because peace is not found in the world, it's found in the Word. Jesus is the Word of God. He is the Prince of Peace, and we can only receive true peace through Jesus.

> In the beginning was the Word, and the Word was with God, and the Word was God. He was in the beginning with God. All things were made through

Him, and without Him nothing was made that was made. (John 1:1–3, NKJV)

He was clothed with a robe dipped in blood, and His name is called The Word of God. (Revelation 19:13, NKJV)

For unto us a Child is born, Unto us a Son is given; And the government will be upon His shoulder. And His name will be called Wonderful, Counselor, Mighty God, Everlasting Father, Prince of Peace. Of the increase of His government and peace there will be no end, Upon the throne of David and over His kingdom, To order it and establish it with judgment and justice from that time forward, even forever. The zeal of the Lord of hosts will perform this. (Isaiah 9:6–7, NKJV)

There is no end to Jesus' peace! We can receive peace in our lives through Jesus Christ the Word that is His own peace. See for yourself.

"These things I have spoken to you, that in Me you may have peace. In the world you will have tribulation; but be of good cheer, I have overcome the world." (John 16:33, NKJV)

Grace, mercy, and peace will be with you from God the Father and from the Lord Jesus Christ, the Son of the Father, in truth and love. (2 John 1:3, NKJV)

For He Himself is our peace, who has made both one, and has broken down the middle wall of separation, (Ephesians 2:14, NKJV)

I learned the power of the Word of God and this important truth when I was about 14 years old. I realized that I needed the Word of God to have peace in my life. Through the tribulation I was facing at that time, I went to the Holy Bible and began to read it. Whenever I faced the opposition, I would turn to the Word. I would read the Holy Bible until the opposition I was facing came to an end.

There were many days that I would just read entire chapters of the Holy Bible. I learned that through Jesus Christ (the Word) I could have peace in my life. I learned that whatever I faced opposite the Word of God could not have victory as long as I had the Word in my life, with Jesus Christ, and the power of His own words, I would overcome. This important truth stuck with me. I had to become more patient going through the tribulation I was facing because the situation I was in didn't change much for a while. But I still could have peace going through it all.

> And not only that, but we also glory in tribulations, knowing that tribulation produces perseverance; and perseverance, character, and character, hope. Now hope does not disappoint, because the love of God has been poured out in our hearts by the Holy Spirit who was given to us. (Romans 5:3–5, NKJV)

Now I wasn't able to glory in my tribulation then, but I am learning to as I depend on Him more and more. Just like the scripture says in Romans 5:3–5, the tribulation produces perseverance, and as we become more patient we build our character, and our character produces hope. It's tough when we have to face the tribulations in life, but we don't have to face them alone! Jesus wants us to depend on Him; we have to trust the Word. As we seek Him and depend on Him, and trust Him, we are able to glory in His name, and glory threw our tribulation.

> Glory in His name; Let the hearts of those rejoice who seek the LORD! Seek the LORD and His strength; Seek His face evermore! (1 Chronicles 16:10–11, NKJV)

Trust the Word!

We can truly have peace in our lives going through the tribulations in life, only when we trust the Word, and not the world. Isn't it awesome that we can trust Him? We can receive peace from Jesus, and we really need it to get through this life. Jesus' peace is not the same as the world's peace; there isn't much peace in the world we live, and we need His peace to live in this world! He left it here for us to receive; obviously, He knew that we were going to need it.

> 'Peace I leave with you, My peace I give to you; not as the world gives do I give to you. Let not your heart be troubled, neither let it be afraid.
>
> (John 14:27, NKJV)

> Now may the Lord of peace Himself give you peace always in every way. The Lord be with you all. (2 Thessalonians 3:16, NKJV)

> But the meek shall inherit the earth, and shall delight themselves in the abundance of peace. (Psalm 37:11, NKJV)

> And let the peace of God rule in your hearts, to
> which also you were called in one body; and be
> thankful. (Colossians 3:15, NKJV)

Sometimes the things that we face in life end up to be burdens. When this happens, Jesus is there to lift it up from us. All we have to do is let the burden go right into His hands, and then we have to believe that He's got a hold of it. The Lord doesn't want us to bear a burden that we cannot bear. That's why He says come to Me all you who are heaven laden (carrying a heavy load) and I will give you rest. Some burdens can be heavy things to carry, and He doesn't expect us to carry what we can't handle.

If the load is too heavy to carry then just let it go! Just trust! But there are times when the Lord wants us to bear a burden. And when He's given us a burden to bear, it will be something light that we can carry. It will be a balanced load. Take the yoke of marriage, the bond that keeps the bride and the bridegroom together, keeping close contact.

This is something that the church can carry, as we keep close contact with our God, loving Him fully hearted and the family that He's set before us. We must know the difference; one is heavy on us, and one is light on us. If it's too heavy, you can cast your cares upon him. And we also must know that the commandments of the Lord are not burdensome.

> "Come to Me, all you who labor and are heavy
> laden, and I will give you rest. "Take My yoke upon
> you and learn from Me, for I am gently and lowly
> in heart, and you will find rest for your souls. "For
> My yoke is easy and My burden is light." (Matthew
> 11:28–30, NKJV)

For this is the love of God, that we keep His commandments. And His commandments are not burden-some. (1 John 5:3, NKJV)

Cast your burden on the LORD, And He shall sustain you; He shall never permit the righteous to be moved. (Psalm 55:22, NKJV)

I learned that even though I was facing tough times in my life, I could have all the peace I needed. I learned to trust the Lord as I was going through my situation and circumstances. When things get tough, they get tough! And even though I have learned to have the peace of God to rule in my heart, life experiences can still be very difficult, and I find that it's in the difficult times that He teaches me. I learn to become more patient for love is patient. I developed a great love for God.

I found my security in Him realizing that He is our Father, and we all are ultimately in His hands, and nothing shall separate us from God's love and His eternal plan!

Who shall separate us from the love of Christ? Shall tribulation, or distress, or persecution, or famine, or nakedness, or peril, or sward? Yet in all these things we are more than conquerors through Him who loved us. For I am persuaded that neither death nor life, nor angels nor principalities nor powers, nor things present, nor things to come, nor height nor depth, nor any other created thing, shall be able to separate us from the love of God which is in Christ Jesus our Lord. (Romans 8:35, 37–39, NKJV)

"And I give them eternal life, and they shall never perish; neither shall anyone snatch them out of My hand. "My Father, who has given them to Me, is greater than all; and no one is able to snatch them out of My Fathers hand. "I and My Father are one." (John 10:28–30, NKJV)

So we may boldly say: "The LORD is my helper; I will not fear. What can man do to me?" (Hebrews 13:6, NKJV)

Life is change awaiting a new season to begin, thanking Him for the feelings within.

Once we are born again, we must go through a life change. We've made it to the starting line, we've started the race that is set before us, and we want to shine our way to the finishing line, so *we must not let sin rule over us*! We are not a corruptible seed! As I said, Jesus came to change us, and now we have to walk into the change that's been given to us through Him who made it possible for us to walk in it. Our life will begin to change like the seasons do in the natural world, and we will grow through each season if we walk according to His Word.

having been born again, not of corruptible seed but incorruptible, through the word of God which lives and abides forever, (1 Peter 1:23, NKJV)

Do all things without complaining and disputing, that you may become blameless and harmless, children of God without fault in the midst of a crooked and perverse generation, among whom you shine as lights in the world, (Philippians 2:14, NKJV)

knowing this, that our old man was crucified with Him, that the body of sin might be done away with, that we should no longer be slaves of sin. For he who has died has been freed from sin. For sin shall not have dominion over you, for you are not under the law but under grace. (Romans 6:6–7, 14, NKJV)

And do not be conformed to this world, but be transformed by the renewing of your mind, that you may prove what is the good and acceptable and perfect will of God. (Romans 12:2, NKJV)

As we make those laps in our life, walking according to His Word, we become a light in the world! People will see the light because the Light is in us and now shines through us onto others. The light that people see is us functioning in our life, just as He did. The next scripture here tells us that as we receive Christ Jesus the Lord, to walk in Him. That means clearly to walk in Him. What is it of Him that we walk in? What about His Spirit! His Light! His Life! His Love!

If we are walking in Him, then people will see Him in us. They will see His light, and we will be able to shine our way to that finishing line!

As you therefore have received Christ Jesus the Lord, so walk in Him, rooted and built up in Him and established in the faith, as you have been taught, abounding in it with thanksgiving. (Colossians 2:6–7, NKJV)

You are all sons of the light and sons of the day. We are not of the night nor of darkness. (1 Thessalonians 5:5, NKJV)

"Let your light so shine before men, that they may see your good works and glorify your Father in heaven. (Matthew 5:16, NKJV)

In these laps we make, we are able to see what's going on around us because God has opened our eyes, and He's given us His Spirit. We are able to see His kingdom, His will, His purposes, and we need to be seeing and hearing through the eyes and ears of God in this world, and not the eyes and ears of the physical world.

> Now we received, not the spirit of the world, but the Spirit who is from God, that we may know the things that have been freely given to us by God. These things we also speak, not in the words which man's wisdom teaches but which the Holy Spirit teaches, comparing spiritual things with spiritual. But the natural man does not receive the things of the Spirit of God, for they are foolishness to him; nor can he know them, because they are spiritually discerned. (1 Corinthians 2:12–14, NKJV)

People try to change themselves, but we must know that we cannot change ourselves, only God can change us. We know many are the plans in our heart, but it is the Lord's purpose that prevails!

<hr />

What Happens When We Are on the Tracks?

When we open up our hearts to God and we walk in obedience to His Word through the Spirit, He changes us from day to day. Our relationship with God grows! God teaches us, we don't just know of God, but we begin to know God. He's something that's worth seeing. It's like we step out of bounds as we are on the track. We aim to seek more of Him. It's not the race the world runs, it's the race that the Church runs! We all want to see Him shining at the finishing line!

We connect with His heart. It's an amazing journey! And when we slip and fall, He still picks us up and dusts us off, and sets us back on the track. As you run this race, don't try and do it alone. Many are running the same race. They are beside you to help you along the way; they are not competing with you, and they want to shine their way to the finishing line as well. It is the household of God who is beside you, and you are in this household. Keep close contact with them along the way. It's likely that they will help you from slipping and falling. He will transform us along the way so that we will be without spot or wrinkle!

We have to look to the Creator who created us in love with purpose and say, God we want You to change us into all that You called us to be. We aren't able Lord. Only You are able, and we want to be God-centered people, not self-centered people.

When we submit to God for His help in us then we won't be focusing on us anymore and what we can do. We'll be focusing on the Creator and what He can do. From glory to glory we will be transformed.

> But we all, with unveiled face, beholding as in a mirror the glory of the Lord, are being transformed into the same image from glory to glory, just as by the Spirit of the Lord. (2 Corinthians 3:18, NKJV)

> Therefore we do not lose heart. Even though our outward man is perishing, yet the inward man is being renewed day by day. (2 Corinthians 4:16, NKJV)

> Now, therefore, you are no longer strangers and foreigners, but fellow citizens with the saints and members of the household of God, having been built on the foundation of the apostles and prophets, Jesus Christ Himself being the chief cornerstone, in whom the whole building, being fitted together, grows into a holy temple in the Lord, in whom you also are being built together for a dwelling place of God in the Spirit. (Ephesians 2:19–22, NKJV)

> that He might present her to Himself a glorious church, not having spot or wrinkle or any such thing, but that she should be holy and without blemish. (Ephesians 5:27, NKJV)

We cannot accomplish the transformation alone, but by His Spirit! We're not the ones who need to be working on our behalf. Why are we working so hard?

All we have to do is follow His plan that works in us and eventually through us. He works on our behalf! Mankind from the beginning is always trying to do things man's way; God wants us to do things His way—a way that is for us and not against us. When we turn to our own ways and the world's way, we must realize it's a plan that will only work against us and will never be a plan fulfilled in righteousness. God's plans have meaning and fulfillment and are done in righteousness. His way is always the right way! Our ways seem right, but many are the plans in a person's heart right?

Our ways are not the right way. Jesus Christ is the way, the truth, and the life! In the beginning, Adam and Eve desired to do what they wanted to do, instead of what God told them not to do. They did not listen to the voice of God and His command. Instead, they listened to the voice of the serpent (temptation) and because of this, sin came into the world. Go God's way and let Him do all the work in you. When we let God work in us, what will happen is, all the work He's done in us will be used for us to give to the people in the world.

God first works in us what we will be able to give to the world around us. As you run the race that is set before you, obey His voice and allow God to work in your life along the way! It first gets worked into us, and then into the world in which we live in. We give to others what was given to us by God. What we give does not come directly from us but directly from God.

Every good and perfect gift is from above, what then do we humans have to give?

God Gave Us His Perfect Gift—His Son!

God gave us His perfect gift, His Son, for us to share with the world, to proclaim the good news of His salvation from day to day! Repentance and remission of sins should be preached in His name to all nations!

> Sing to the LORD, all the earth; Proclaim the good news of His salvation from day to day. Declare His glory among the nations, His wonders among all peoples. (1 Chronicles 16:23–24, NKJV)

> Then He said to them, "Thus it is written, and thus it was necessary for the Christ to suffer and to rise from the dead the third day, "and that repentance and remission of sins should be preached in His

name to all nations, beginning at Jerusalem. (Luke 24:46–47, NKJV)

I'm declaring the good news of His salvation from day to day. I'm declaring His glory among the nations, His wonders among all peoples. How about you? We (all the earth) are to sing to the Lord and to proclaim the good news of His salvation from day to day. That is what the Lord expects us to be giving to all people, and (it's the message of the "Good News about His Son, Jesus Christ)" the best message that we could ever give is the one that is of the "Good News." The Gospel of Jesus Christ! It's the power of God, and it's only foolishness to those who are perishing. Jesus is a free gift to the world. Proclaim the message of the "Good News" of His salvation from day to day!

> For the message of the cross is foolishness to those who are perishing, but to us who are being saved it is the power of God. (1 Corinthians 1:18, NKJV)

God has set you on the track with a message! Shout it loud and proud! It doesn't matter what age we enter this race. Whether we are young or old, He's the one who brought us to the starting line and expects us to run the race that's set before us, and He will get us to the finishing line! People need to hear some good news. You have it to give to them! God wants us to be a giving people, a people who give with a cheerful heart. Where not giving to people what we have to give, we are giving to people what He has to give.

It all belongs to the Mighty One! When someone comes our way and has a need of what we have and asks us, then we should give with a cheerful heart. Even if they don't ask us, we can see a need and help meet it for someone! That's a cheerful heart! One who loves to give!

> "Give to everyone who asks of you. And from Him who takes away your goods do not ask them back. "Give, and it will be given to you: good measure, pressed down, shaken together, and running over will be put into your bosom. For with the same measure you use, it will be measured back to you." (Luke 6:30, 38, NKJV)

> So let each one give as he purposes in his heart, not grudgingly or of necessity; for God loves a cheerful giver. (2 Corinthians 9:7, NKJV)

When we trust, we don't hold onto things! We aren't taking any of it with us, so give it!

God has made me a cheerful giver. I loved seeing the reaction of people when they say, "Hey, I like that," and I just give it to them. We aren't used to this. We guard our possessions and treasure them, but not one thing will go with us except for the gifts that God has put inside of us. These are the gifts we get to keep, so why treasure our possessions?

You might think that you have nothing to give to people, but you could never show up anywhere empty-handed. People could never come to you, and you have nothing to give to them because we carry our gifts within us. We never come empty-handed. He's put it all in our hands to give out. We have blessed hands. Jesus Christ doesn't show up empty-handed! On earth, He used His own hands to bless people. He healed people, gave sight to the blind, turned water into wine; we know He did many other miracles, but the greatest thing that I believe He ever did was give His love and compassion for all.

When Jesus died on the cross His arms were wide open to the whole world as He was saying I love the whole world so much that I give My life for you all. And at the ascension, He lifted His hands to bless His own. He said, in Matthew 28:20 (NKJV) "And lo, I am with you always, even to the end of the age." Amen.

He's with us when we start the race, as we run the race, and even at the finish line. His arms are always open to give a hug of comfort, to pray on our behalf, to bless us still, to heal us, to love us, and to guide us. And He fulfills with His own hand all that He's spoken and all His purposes prevail!

Our Helper!

God works through us. He's called us to be a part of His plans and purpose. He truly loves mankind, His special creation. Don't forget the Helper in you, The Holy Spirit is your Helper and teacher. He lives in you and gets you to the finishing line. Seek after those things which are above, set your mind on things above!

> If then you were raised with Christ, seek those things which are above, where Christ is, sitting at the right hand of God. Set your mind on things above, not on things on the earth. (Colossians 3:1–2, NKJV)

We have to seek those things which are above and set our mind on things above! We have to live according to the Spirit of truth that gives us life. We should not only seek Him in our times of need. We should seek Him whatever the circumstance may be. He guides us into all truth. We are born of heaven and thus heaven approved!

Our new birth separates us from the rest of the world and the world itself. We are children of the Father, isn't that cool? We are in the household of God! The new born-again life is able to live forever and will never die because it was given eternal life through Jesus Christ the Lord. The new born-again life must now walk in the Spirit that it was given and not the flesh that it was originally born into; our flesh will never please God. And let's face it, it doesn't please others either. We belong to Him in heaven above and on the earth also. We are His!

> So then, those who are in the flesh cannot please God. (Romans 8:8, NKJV)

> By this we know that we abide in Him, and He in us, because He has given us of His Spirit. (1 John 4:13, NKJV)

> For if you live according to the flesh you will die; but if by the Spirit you put to death the deeds of the body, you will live. For as many as are led by the Spirit of God, these are the sons of God. The Spirit Himself bears witness with our spirit that we are children of God. (Romans 8:13–14, 16, NKJV)

> And the Lord will deliver me from every evil work and preserve me for His heavenly kingdom. To Him be glory forever and ever. Amen. (2 Timothy 4:18, NKJV)

> Also we need to put on the whole armor of God and also wear the armor of light.

The night is far spent, the day is at hand. Therefore let us cast off the works of darkness, and let us put on the armor of light. (Romans 13:12, NKJV)

Therefore take up the whole armor of God, that you may be able to withstand in the evil day, and having done all, to stand. Stand therefore, having girded your waist with truth, having put on the breastplate of righteousness, and having shod your feet with the preparation of the gospel of peace; above all, taking the shield of faith with which you will be able to quench all the fiery darts of the wicked one. And take the helmet of salvation, and the sward of the Spirit, which is the word of God; praying always with all prayer and supplication in the Spirit, being watchful to this end with all perseverance and supplication for all the saints- (Ephesians 6:13–18, NKJV)

Life is not worried about the days ahead. Life is lived by the leading of the Spirit instead.

"Therefore do not worry about tomorrow, for tomorrow will worry about its own things. Sufficient for the day is its own trouble. (Matthew 6:34, NKJV)

It's easy for us to worry about everything in our lives, especially in the times we are living in now. With all the natural disasters and attacks, our economy issues, global warming, arctic freezing, war, and uncertainties, it can all be overwhelming at times. We need to not forget His covenant. It is the covenant that we have with Him that gives us restoration. If we want to be a blessed nation that blesses nations, we must be in agreement with God. He's the One who restores! Sometimes we forget that God is bigger than our problems.

We forget that He's the solution. We must let God be God and trust Him! He is in control! He has an eternal plan! His ways are not our ways! He says and it is! He has given us His own peace, and it never ends. Let His peace rule in your heart, and do not doubt His covenant. He promises blessings for those who live by it. We also live in a fast-paced society. We're trying to fill up our days full of tomorrow's events.

Let's take it one day at a time, the load will be lighter that way. One day alone keeps our hands full enough, and we can't run laps with multiple loads. When we get tired, take a break and walk; let's not wear ourselves out. If were running this race too fast, and we are all worn out, we'll miss what's on the sidelines. People need us! Also, let's not forget that we are not competing!

People are hungry for what we have for them. We are carrying baskets of fruit; we have to carry it gently. The Spirit is gentle, He will get us to the finishing line on time and along the way, our fruit will remain. It will feed the hungry souls! The Father knows all the things we will ever need, and we are to not worry about a thing. So why are we? Why are we piling days upon days?

We have to start letting the day be the day, and trust God knowing that He's in control of it all.

> "And when you pray, do not use vain repetitions as the heathen do, For they think they will be heard for their many words. "Therefore do not be like them. For your Father knows the things you have need of before you ask Him. "In this manner, therefore, pray: Our Father in heaven, Hallowed be Your name. Your

kingdom come. Your will be done on earth as it is in heaven. Give us this day our daily bread. And forgive us our debts, As we forgive our debtors. And do not lead us into temptation, But deliver us from the evil one. For Yours is the kingdom and the power and the glory forever. Amen. (Matthew 6:7–13, NKJV)

"Therefore do not worry, saying, 'What shall we eat?' or 'What shall we drink?' or 'What shall we wear?' "For after all these things the Gentiles seek. For your heavenly Father knows that you need all these things. "But seek first the kingdom of God and His righteousness, and all these things shall be added to you. "Therefore do not worry about tomorrow, for tomorrow will worry about it's own things. Sufficient for the day is it's own trouble. (Matthew 6:31–34, NKJV)

We can rely on the Spirit of truth, the Holy Spirit, to guide us through our day. And when we focus on Jesus, putting Him first in our lives, then everything else just falls into its place. Meditating on the word of God is an awesome replacement for worrying. We can just meditate on the word of God and even the good things in life instead of worrying about everything.

"Which of you by worrying can add one cubit to his stature? (Matthew 6:27, NKJV)

Finally, brethren, whatever things are true, whatever things are noble, whatever things are just, whatever things are pure, whatever things are lovely, whatever things are of a good report, if there is any virtue and if there is anything praiseworthy-meditate on these things. (Philippians 4:8, NKJV)

Oh, how I love Your law! It is my meditation all the day. (Psalm 119:97, NKJV)

When we seek for God to rule and reign in our lives, God will add to our lives all the things that we have need of.

"But seek first the kingdom of God and His righteousness, and all these things shall be added to you. (Matthew 6:33, NKJV)

This is not always easy for us to do but can be accomplished with the help of the Holy Spirit in us and with great faith in knowing the Creator and trusting Him! We just replace worry with trust, that's all. If we want to get through the day, we have to live by the leading of the Holy Spirit, instead of worrying.

4

Handcrafted by His Love

Life is the art of God's work, handcrafted by His love for the world.

I don't know if anyone will be able to experience all of the wonders that are here on the earth; there is so much to see. From every mountain, hill, and valley, from every ocean, river and stream, from every tree, plant and grassland, from every watered creature to every bird, from every living creature to every creeping thing, from every person—none is the same. From the top of the sky to the bottom, to everything small and great, everywhere and everything is glorious. From glory to glory He's made it all! It's all His! He said and it became so, and out of it all what He loves most is you and I, His people.

None of us is exactly alike. Nobody is like you, and we are all a work of His art. I thank the Lord that I am a masterpiece, a work of His art, and you can too. He made everything perfect for us to enjoy. I try to enjoy everything that God has made as much as I can. There was a time in my life when I never use to pay much attention to what was in the world as I was growing up in it, it just was natural to me.

I never stopped to look at just exactly what was around me. I never realized what was so natural said so much about the Creator. I never realized it all had a purpose. I never realized it was all made because He had a special creation in mind. You and I, His people.

The truth of the matter is, when I finally stopped to look at what was around me, I realized that it's quite amazing. I never realized how much is really out there around us. If you haven't realized it yet, you can realize it now. Get off the couch, get out of the bed, get up, and get out there and start exploring!

Life is full of miracles from God alone. We are all one of His own. As we look out into our world we can clearly see how life is a miracle to us. Everything that God created is so amazing! What an awesome God we have. We can especially understand how miraculous life is by watching a human life stage in its development in the world. It amazes me how a child grows and becomes an adult.

With my own children, I'm learning not to make-or-break them in the development process. In other words, I don't want to make my kids what I want them to be, or break them of what I don't want them to be. The thing that we sometimes forget to realize is that God is the One who made them, and God is the One who's going to get them to the starting line and ultimately bring them to the full and mature place that He's called them to be. We have to trust the Lord!

His Love Made Us!

We understand that a man and woman's love is what makes a child, but really this only plays a part in God's plans. I think of it like this: *God's love made me, and His love made you.* He first loved us, and His love is what made us. Remember God is love, and God gives love. So we all became because God first loved, then man and woman fulfill His purpose in love.

A mother and father's role is to raise the children and bring them to a place of maturity, by teaching them according to the word of God. When we are born again, we have become children of God, and have begun childhood all over again.

> Then Jesus called a little child to Him, set him in the midst of them, and said, "Assuredly, I say to you, unless you are converted and become as little children, you will by no means enter the kingdom of heaven. (Matthew 18:2–3, NKJV)

> But as many as received Him, to them He gave the right to become children of God, to those who believe in His name. (John 1:12, NKJV)

God made us His children not that we should stay children, but that as we walk in obedience to His Word and His Spirit, Father God's plan is to bring us to full maturity. As we rear our children to be the best individuals they can be, our words and actions to them are very important as well.

Let no corrupt word proceed out of your mouth, but
what is good for necessary edification, that it may
impart grace to the hearers. (Ephesians 4:29, NKJV)

Train a child in the way he should go, and when he is
old he will not depart from it. (Proverbs 22:6, NKJV)

When we think about our children, we should
understand that they became because God loved first, and
they belong to Him. We are raising them for God's purposes.
And when our children are born again, they too will be
converted and become His children. God will ultimately
bring them into full maturity. We can look at this process
and understand that it's not to make-or-break them along
the way. It's the process of teaching them according to the
word of God for His purposes.

As we are walking examples of His Word, our children
will learn from us to be a walking example of His Word as
well. Our children will learn to walk by His Word as we
walk by His Word. We need to be walking in obedience to
the word of God and not follow the disobedience of the
world. If we are walking in obedience to His Word, our
children will not likely be following the disobedience of the
world, they will more likely be following in our footsteps
that are His footsteps. They are with us on the tracks, and
the race that is set before us that we run is their learning
experience. When they begin to run their own race, they
will have the life experiences they have learned according
to God's word as part of their mature being. We can see
what a miracle it is for us to receive a second birth that will
allow us to live according to His Word in the world, and
ultimately with Jesus forever in eternity!

Understanding the stages of this birth process is miraculous; it's only possible because of Father's love and His plans, and purposes for His Son and us, and His Son fulfilling His purposes in love for the Father and us.

> Let all that you do be done with love. (1 Corinthians 16:14, NKJV)

Life is a song our heart sings. Life is praising Jesus the King.

> Speaking to one another in psalms and hymns and spiritual songs, singing and making melody in our heart to the Lord. (Ephesians 5:19, NKJV)

Our life is like a song sung to the Lord when we live our lives by the Word of God and follow Jesus. Our whole life should praise Jesus the King! Everything about us should praise the Lord, for He is merciful, and

His mercy endures forever. Everything that God created should praise Him—that means everything, we all should! He deserves to be praised. He's a King! The King of all kings, and we are His princes and princesses. Praise Him! We are a royal Priesthood!

Everything we do in our daily life can praise God if our heart is in the right place. We should praise the Lord even for the air we breathe, for life alone. He's worthy!

> I will sing to the Lord as long as I live; I will sing praise to my God while I have my being. (Psalm 104:33, NKJV)

Praise the Lord! Praise the Lord from the heavens, Praise Him in the heights; Praise Him, all His angels; Praise Him, all His hosts; Praise Him, sun and moon; Praise him, all you stars of light! Praise Him, you heavens of heavens; and waters above the heavens! Let them praise the name of the Lord, For He commanded and they were created. He also established them forever and ever; He made a decree which shall not pass away. Praise the Lord from the earth, You great sea creatures and all the depths; Fire and hail, snow and clouds; Stormy wind, fulfilling His word; Mountains and all hills; Fruitful trees and all cedars; Beasts and all cattle; Creeping things and flying fowl; Kings of the earth and all peoples; Princes and all judges of the earth; Both young men and maidens; Old men and children. Let them praise the name of the Lord, For His name alone is exalted; His glory is above the earth and heaven. And He has exalted the horn of His people, the praise of all His saints- Of the children of Israel, A people near to Him. Praise the LORD! (Psalm 148, NKJV)

See, everything that God created has a part in praising Him. We think it's easy to praise God when our lives are going great, but we should praise God even when our life isn't going so great. This is not so hard to do, you know. I know when it gets tough, it gets tough, right? It's tough.

But even in pain, I still lift my hands to the Lord. Sometimes I just rest at His feet, knowing that He is able to help me. I don't let go of the promise, His Word; I hold it in my heart, and it becomes my song to Him. Sometimes I can only hum, but my heart still sings the tune, and the Lord is always faithful—He will be to the end. Having

Jesus in your heart, you have the ability to sing a heartfelt song to Him.

He will give us the greatest strength when we praise Him in our times of trouble, because He will prevail, and we will overcome through His strength. Isn't that comforting to know that even in our weakness, He is our strength, and in times of troubles we can overcome with His strength. Through our praises we can receive His strength to overcome, that's awesome! Glory be to God! One of the greatest ways that we can praise God in times of troubles is by singing to the Lord. When we sing to the Lord with all of our heart, we can give glory to God. Singing to the Lord releases a lot of anxiety, and it will bless us. We can receive so much simply by just praising the living God with all of our heart.

> Let the word of Christ dwell in you richly in all wisdom, teaching and admonishing one another in psalms and hymns and spiritual songs, singing with grace in your hearts to the Lord. (Colossians 3:16, NKJV)

> The Lord is my strength and my song, And He has become my salvation; He is my God, and I will praise Him; (Exodus 15:2, NKJV)

Sing a song of praise and purpose to the Lord!

Life is thanking Him for the taste and smell of food that we eat. Life is full of flavors so neat.

I love food! I love that God created us to desire to eat food and have a need for food. It amazes me how much food God created for us to eat. I love the colors of fruits and vegetables. I love herbs, and olives, natural oils, grains and nuts. I love the shapes and textures and different sizes, the smell and taste also. I'm probably a lot like you when it comes to food. I love cooking and experimenting with food, it's so fun. I love to eat the food that God created, I just like the crisp fresh natural taste of God-made food.

I'm amazed of all the different nutrients it provides in order to keep the body healthy, and all of its benefits. The more I learn about what God has made, the more I learn about God. All the colors He likes, I'm focusing on food here, there are so many different kinds; they are all different colors, sizes, shapes, smells, textures, and it all has a purpose. God gave us our senses to experience it all, and I love that God has revealed Himself in creation and through His Word (Jesus Christ). When we read the Bible, the Word of God, it reveals Jesus Christ to us. Reading the Bible is important like eating food.

> Then God said, "Let the land produce vegetation: seed-bearing plants and trees on the land that bear fruit with seed in it, according to their various kinds." And it was so. The land produced vegetation: plants bearing seed according to their kinds and trees bearing fruit with seed in it according to their kinds. And God saw that it was good. (Genesis 1:11–12, NIV)

> How sweet are Your words to my taste, sweeter than honey to my mouth! (Psalm 119:103, NKJV)

> But Jesus answered him, saying, "It is written, 'Man shall not live by bread alone, but by every word of God.'" (Luke 4:4, NKJV)

> "It is the Spirit who gives life; the flesh profits nothing. The words that I speak to you are spirit, and they are life. (John 6:63, NKJV)

Sometimes I eat and read the Bible at the same time. I think it is awesome that we can feed our body and spirit at the same time, not forgetting our soul too. He feeds as we see how much He really does love mankind, His special creation. I'm thankful that the Lord feeds us of His own self also.

> And Jesus said to them, "I am the bread of life. He who comes to Me shall never hunger, and he who believes in Me shall never thirst. "I am the bread of life. "This is the bread which comes down from heaven, that one may eat of it and not die. "I am the living bread which came down from heaven. If anyone eats of this bread, he will live forever; and the bread that I shall give is My flesh, which I shall give for the life of the world."(John 6:35, 48, 50–51, NKJV)

> Who gives food to all flesh, for His mercy endures forever. Oh give thanks to the God of heaven! For His mercy endures forever. (Psalm 136:25–26, NKJV)

See, God had desired for us to enjoy our food; He gave us plenty of it to eat. Let's review that again. He's given us food for our physical body. He's given us food for our spirit that is the Word of God. He's given us food for our soul that is fed by His love, and the love we receive from others. He's definitely supplied all the food we need to feed our whole being. That's why it's important for us to be feeding our whole being. Food for our body just isn't all that we need.

This is only stage 1, I'll call it.
Stages 2 and 3 are even better!
Now just think about it. Stage #1: Body.
How do you feel when you don't eat food for your body?
Do you get weak? Of course you do! That's because we need it to survive.

> Then God said, "Let the earth bring forth grass, the herb that yields seed, and the fruit tree that yields fruit according to its kind, whose seed is in itself, on the earth"; and it was so. And God said, "See, I have given you every herb that yields seed which is on the face of all the earth, and every tree whose fruit yields seed; to you it shall be for food. (Genesis 1:11, 29, NKJV)

> "Every moving thing that lives shall be for food for you. I have given you all things, even as the green herbs. "But you shall not eat flesh with its life, that is, its blood. (Genesis 9:3–4, NKJV)

> When He had called all the multitude to Himself, He said to them, "Hear Me, everyone, and understand: "There is nothing that enters a man from outside which can defile him; but the things which come out of him, those are the things that defile a man. "If anyone has ears to hear, let him hear!" So He said to them, "Are you thus without understanding also? Do you not perceive that whatever enters a man from the outside cannot defile him, "because it does not enter his heart but his stomach, and is eliminated, thus purifying all foods?" (Mark 7:14–16, 18–19, NKJV)

Now what about love?

Stage #2: Soul.

Do you get a little weak when you don't feel loved? Of course you do. We were created to love and be loved. If we're not getting the love that we need, our soul would starve. But it doesn't have to because Jesus loves us all. He has love for you, and all you have to do is receive it!

> If you extend your soul to the hungry and satisfy the afflicted soul, Then your light shall dawn in the darkness, And your darkness shall be as the noonday. The Lord will guide you continually, And satisfy your soul in drought, And strengthen your bones; You shall be like a watered garden, And like a spring of water, whose waters do not fail. (Isaiah 58:10–11, NKJV)

What about the Word of God?

Stage #3-Spirit.

How do you think this affects our being?

Do you know that your spirit needs the Word of God to have life? All of you need's the Word of God to have life!

> "It is the Spirit who gives life; the flesh profits nothing. The words that I speak to you are spirit, and they are life. (John 6:63, NKJV)

> But Jesus answered him, saying, "It is written, Man shall not live by bread alone, but by every word of God.'" (Luke 4:4, NKJV)

Jesus said whoever comes to Him will never hunger or thirst, so we are able to go to His Word daily; He will feed us from it and fill us. See, we don't get full by reading the

Word of God just once, we should go to it every day for our daily bread. We certainly wouldn't get full if we only ate one meal a day either for our body, nor would we get full of love if only one person loved us. Jesus is the only person who can fill us full of His love! God created us for relationships, and He has given us the whole body of Christ to feed us. With that, we need to extend our soul to others, we need each other and need Him.

God wants us to have relationships with people, and if we want to receive love from others, we have to first give it. We need people in our lives! And people need us! He's given us a big family, His family. We are a part of the household of God!

See, every part is important for our being. We need all the stages of food for survival! We may be living on only stage 1, if you will, but truly ask yourself, do you feel a little weak? See, we're missing out if we are only eating of stage #1. No wonder we get weak sometimes, we have to be fed by all that God has given us to eat; we need it to survive. We truly need His love and we have to reciprocate. We need to give love to others and receive love from others.

> "'And you shall love the Lord your God with all your heart, with all your soul, with all your mind, and with all your strength.' This is the first commandment. "And the second, like it, is this: 'You shall love your neighbor as yourself.' There is no other commandment greater than these." (Mark 12:30–31, NKJV)

Jesus also gave us a new commandment.

> "A new commandment I give to you, that you love one another as I have loved you, that you also love one another. "By this all will know that you are My disciples, if you have love for one another." (John 13:34–35, NKJV)

> "This is My commandment, that you love one another as I have loved you. (John 15:12, NKJV)

> "These things I command you, that you love one another. (John 15:17, NKJV)

We need His love to reach the world. Our love goes with us to eternity. Remember, love never ends. We truly need the Word of God! The Word is the beginning and the end. We need Jesus Christ the Word of God, or we don't have life. God's Word will never pass away; it's eternal!

> He was clothed with a robe dipped in blood, and His name is called The Word of God. (Revelation 19:13 NKJV)

> And He has on His robe and on His thigh a name written: KING OF KINGS AND LORD OF LORDS. (Revelation 19:16, NKJV)

> "I am the Alpha and the Omega, the Beginning and the End," says the Lord, "who is and who was and who is to come, the Almighty." (Revelation 1:8, NKJV)

Can you see that Jesus Christ, the Word of God and His love, is eternally necessary for our being? If we're only eating food needed for our body to survive, what does that tell you? It tells me that the only thing it eventually gains is a little weight. This is because our being is really craving the rest of the other stages. It's like a car trying to go on a long journey with only a quarter tank of gas.

"We need to be on full" if we're going to make the journey of life. A car wouldn't make it on a quarter tank of gas for a long journey, neither will we. We all want to make the journey, and it's long, we better fill up and press on! We need the headlight to lead us and be on full! We need to remember what Jesus' main food was (to do the will of the Father who sent Him, and to finish His work).

> But He said to them, "I have food to eat of which you do not know." Therefore the disciples said to one another, "Has anyone brought Him anything to eat?" Jesus said to them, "My food is to do the will of Him who sent Me, and to finish His work. (John 4:32–34, NKJV)

Jesus told His disciples not to labor for the food, which perishes, but for the food that endures to everlasting life— Him! We are to do His work, proclaiming the good news of His salvation from day to day! We are to believe in Jesus and feed the people with His Word. The word of God will feed all those who hunger and thirst.

> "Do not labor for food which perishes, but for the food which endures to everlasting life, which the Son of Man will give you, because God the Father has sent

His seal on Him." Then they said to Him, "What shall we do, that we may work the works of God?"

Jesus answered and said to them, "This is the work of God, that you believe in Him whom He sent."(John 6:27–29, NKJV)

Blessed are those who hunger and thirst for righteousness, For they shall be filled. (Matthew 5:6, NKJV)

Repent and believe in the gospel!

Now after John was put in prison, Jesus came to Galilee, preaching the gospel of the kingdom of God, and saying, "The time is fulfilled, and the kingdom of God is at hand. Repent, and believe in the gospel." (Mark 1:14–15, NKJV)

Jesus didn't seek after His own will; He fulfilled His Father's purpose.

Saying, "Father, if it is Your will, take this cup away from Me; nevertheless not My will, but Yours, be done." (Luke 22:42, NKJV)

"I can of Myself do nothing. As I hear, I judge; and My judgment is righteous, because I do not seek My own will but the will of the Father who sent Me. (John 5:30, NKJV)

"But that the world may know that I love the Father, and as the Father gave Me commandment, so I do. Arise, let us go from here. (John 14:31, NKJV)

When Jesus came to us, He faced it all. When Jesus Christ came to the hour of His life, do you know what happened? We know He faced all difficulty, all suffering, and all pain. He even asked His Father if it was His Father's will to take the cup away from Him, but it wasn't His Father's will to take it away, and Jesus knew that. He said, "Nevertheless not My will, but Yours be done." The hour came so that the Son of Man should be glorified, and Jesus said it was for this purpose He came to this hour.

And He said, "Father glorify Your name."

> But Jesus answered them, saying, "The hour has come that the Son of Man should be glorified. (John 12:23, NKJV)

> "Now My soul is troubled, and what shall I say? "Father, save Me from this hour"? But for this purpose I have come to this hour. "Father, glorify Your name." (John 12:27–28, NKJV)

God was glorified, and Jesus Christ was glorified. And guess what? When our hour comes, God will be glorified too, and so will we. Jesus Christ did not seek His own will, we must not also. Jesus Christ came to preach the gospel, to preach the Kingdom of God and He told His disciples to do the same.

> And He said to them, "Go into all the world and preach the gospel to every creature. "He who believes and is baptized will be saved; but he who does not believe will be condemned. (Mark 16:15–16, NKJV)

> "The Spirit of the Lord is upon Me, Because He has anointed Me To preach the gospel to the poor; He

has sent Me to heal the brokenhearted, To proclaim
liberty to the captives And recovery of sight to the
blind, To set at liberty those who are oppressed; To
proclaim the acceptable year of the LORD." (Luke
4:18–19, NKJV)

But He said to them, "I must preach the kingdom of
God to the other cities also, because for this purpose
I have been sent." (Luke 4:43, NKJV)

And we know that Jesus Christ also came as a light into
the world. Jesus is glorious, and He is the greatest light.

"I have come as a light into the world, that whoever
believes in me should not abide in darkness. (John
12:46, NKJV)

Whatever you are facing in your own life, you might
think nothing good would come from it, but all things
work together for good for those who love God and are
called according to His purposes. In your situation, you can
learn, and it will benefit you later on. Allow God to work in
your heart through your tough times and mature you. If you
do this, God will set you on a hill and you won't be hidden;
you'll shine as a city.

A Family Knit as One in Love

Life is imparting His love into one's hand. He gave His
love to share and expand.

Jesus is worthy to be praised for what He has done for
mankind. He laid down His own life for us all. He truly

loves mankind. He truly loves His Father so much that He obeyed Him, and His will for His life.

> "Now My soul is troubled, and what shall I say? "Father, save Me from this hour"? But for this purpose I came to this hour. "Father, glorify Your name." Then a voice came from heaven, saying, "I have both glorified it and will glorify it again." (John 12:27–28, NKJV)

> "But that the world may know that I love the Father, and as the Father gave Me commandment, so I do. Arise, let us go from here. (John 14:31, NKJV)

> "I am the good shepherd. The good shepherd gives His life for the sheep. (John 10:11, NKJV)

> By this we know love, because He laid down His life for us. And we also ought to lay down our lives for the brethren. (1 John 3:16, NKJV)

> "As the Father loved Me, I also have loved you; abide in My love. (John 15:9, NKJV)

I think it's so amazing that God is so full of love that He gives His love. God gave us His only precious Son, Jesus. He truly loves mankind that He would do this for us all.

> "Therefore My Father loves Me, because I lay down My life that I may take it again. "No one takes My life from Me, but I lay it down of Myself. I have power to lay it down, and I have power to take it

again. This command I have received from My
Father. (John 10:17, NKJV)

"For God so loved the world that He gave His only
begotten Son, that whoever believes in Him should
not perish but have everlasting life. "For God did
not send His Son into the world to condemn the
world, but that the world through Him might be
saved. (John 3:16–17, NKJV)

When we were born into the world, we were pretty
much alone or lonely; until we met Jesus, that is. People
that don't know Jesus are so lonely, and they don't know
why. They get married and find that they are often still
lonely. They have children, and find they are often still
lonely. They could have all their desires and still find that
they are lonely. God created us to long for His only Son,
Jesus Christ.

He is the true love of our life and the relationship we
desire. Have you found what you've been missing in your
life? If you have, don't let go of Him! Our spouse can't fill
our love for Him, Our children can't fill our love for Him,
material things can't fill our love for Him, and money can't
fill our love for Him, only He can fill our love for Him! He
is everything you've been looking for.

A relationship with Jesus is awesome because He
abides in us and we abide in Him, we are never alone! That
is awesome!

"Abide in Me and I in You. As the branch cannot
bear fruit of itself, unless it abides in the vine,
neither can you, unless you abide in Me. "I am the
vine, you are the branches. He who abides in Me,

and I in him, bears much fruit; for without Me you can do nothing. (John 15:4–5, NKJV)

"that they all may be one, as You, Father, are in Me, and I in You; that they also may be one in Us, that the world may believe that You sent Me. "And the glory which You gave Me I have given them, that they may be one just as We are one: "I in them, and You in Me; that they may be made perfect in one, and that the world may know that you sent Me, and have loved them as You have loved Me. "And I have declared to them Your name, and will declare it, that the love with which You loved Me may be in them, and I in them." (John 17:21–23, 26, NKJV)

Life is about experiencing God's love, walking in it, and imparting it to others. There is enough of Jesus' love for everyone. We must share His love with others in need of it.

—⁓⁓∘◦❦◦◦∘⁓⁓—

Our Family

Life is a family knit together as one, Something the Father prepared through the Son

Life is all about being a part of the family of God, being in His household. We know that we were not created in this world to be lonely. God has given us a big family. We must realize that God wants all of us to be a part of His family. Isn't that special of us? His sons and daughters to be called His own? Isn't it awesome that He is our Daddy, and that He would give us brothers and sisters? I think it's awesome!

Most Christians have experienced rejection, whether by their own family or friends or the world. In some way or another, we have felt it. We must realize that we are not rejected by God! It should only matter to us that He's chosen us and called us by our name that we would be a part of His family, His own household.

> "If you were of the world, the world would love its own. Yet because you are not of the world, but I chose you out of the world, therefore the world hates you. (John 15:19, NKJV)

> "To him the doorkeeper opens, and the sheep hear His voice, and he calls His own sheep by name and leads them out. (John 10:3, NKJV)

Once we are born into God's family, we don't have to continue feeling rejected. We finally belong where we were created, in the Father's hands. We are His, not the world's, so rejection shouldn't matter to us anymore.

> Even there Your hand shall lead me, and Your right hand shall hold me. (Psalm 139:10, NKJV)

Jesus faced rejection more than us all will ever, but that didn't seem to affect His identity. Jesus knew who He was, and He knew He belonged to His Father. He knew where He came from (heaven) and where He would return. Once we understand who we are (children of the most High God) and that we belong to Father God, and we are a part of His Kingdom, then we should have confidence in our identity too. We should no longer let the world's rejection keep hindering us from the Father's purpose in our lives.

Jesus didn't let anything keep Him from fulfilling His purpose in life! Rejection is a tough issue to deal with; it's painful. But let's forgive so that we can walk in the purposes

God has set for us. God has a family for us to work in unity with. We need to come to the place of knowing the Lord as He is and knowing each other. We need to walk in a greater level of love for God and others. Remember, God is love, and He gives His love.

We need to grab hold of all the love God has given us so that we can give it to others who are desperately seeking it. And the love that God has given to us, we need to be giving it back to Him; He deserves our love for Him. He wants us to love Him and know Him as He is. God deserves our love. He created us, and without Him we wouldn't be alive or even know Him. God wants us to know Him; He hasn't hidden Himself to be a secret. He has revealed Himself through Jesus Christ, the Word, and creation. He has revealed Himself to us more than we can imagine. He is our family, He will never stop loving us, and He wants our main relationship to be with Him. We can clearly know that He is love. He will not abandon us. He chose us as His children. We are His!

We are His family. We must start to love God with our whole being (body, soul, and spirit).

> 'And you shall love the Lord your God with all your heart, with all your soul, with all your mind, with all your strength.' This is the first commandment. (Mark 12:30, NKJV)

5

Living by the Successor

The Way of Escape

Sin makes us feel like we are in prison, whether or not we are serving a sentence in prison; people today are in prison living in sin. Sin makes us feel enclosed and confined. It brings darkness in our lives. When Adam and Eve sinned, they felt ashamed, and they covered and hid themselves, they were separated from God. How do you feel when you are in sin?

Did you ever feel like there was no way of escape? Did you ever want to hide yourself from it? The only way of escaping this prison is through Jesus Christ, the one who paid the price for our sins. We are able to be free through Him! We cannot hide from Him. If we commit a sin, we need to repent, and He will cleanse us from all unrighteousness.

The feeling of being freed from this kind of prison is like a transformation from darkness to light and life.

We should not abide in darkness anymore! The Lord has turned our darkness into light, and we are His lamp! We are light in the Lord and should walk as children of light. God has a chosen generation to be a royal priesthood, a holy nation, His own special people, a generation to proclaim the praises of Him who called us out of darkness into His marvelous light.

"I have come as a light into the world, that whoever believes in Me should not abide in darkness. (John 12:46, NKJV)

The LORD is my light and my salvation, whom shall I fear? The LORD is the strength of my life; Of whom shall I be afraid? (Psalm 27:1, NKJV)

You are my lamp, O LORD; the LORD turns my darkness into light. (2 Samuel 22:29, NIV)

For you were once darkness, but now you are light in the Lord. Walk as children of light. (Ephesians 5:8, NKJV)

But you are a chosen generation, a royal priesthood, a holy nation, His own special people, that you may proclaim the praises of Him who called you out of darkness into His marvelous light; (1 Peter 2:9, NKJV)

Life is not ruled by the lesser, It is lived by the successor. We know that the sun is the greater light, and the moon, the lesser light; it is the sun that illuminates both. Likewise, Jesus is like the sun, but He is the greatest light of all and our lives reflect His light in our life, He is the greatest light in our life!

> Then God made two great lights: the greater light to rule the day, and the lesser light to rule the night. He made the stars also. (Genesis 1:16, NKJV)

> That was the true Light which gives light to every man coming into the world. (John 1:9, NKJV)

> "I have come as a light into the world, that whoever believes in Me should not abide in darkness. (John 12:46, NKJV)

Knowing that we are light in the Lord, we don't follow the way of the world as we once did. We don't love the things in the world, the lusts of the flesh, the lusts of the eye, and the pride of life. We love The Lord Jesus Christ who is not of this world but of the Kingdom of God, the kingdom in which we now belong. Jesus reigns as King in our hearts and lives! Follow the way of the Word!

> In which you used to live when you followed the way of this world and of the ruler of the kingdom of the air, the spirit who is now at work in those who are disobedient. (Ephesians 2:2, NIV)

> "For what profit is it to a man if he gains the whole world, and loses his own soul? Or what will a man give in exchange for his soul? (Matthew 16:26, NKJV)

> Do not love the world or the things in the world. If anyone loves the world, the love of the Father is

not in him. For all that is in the world—the lusts of the flesh, the lust of the eyes, and the pride of life—is not of the Father but is of the world. (1 John 2:15–16, NKJV)

Jesus answered, "My kingdom is not of this world. If My kingdom were of this world, My servant would fight, so that I should not be delivered to the Jews; but now My kingdom is not from here." (John 18:36, NKJV)

"nor will they say, 'See here!' or 'See there!' For indeed, the kingdom of God is within you." (Luke 17:21, NKJV)

We can't have life if we live by the way of the world, because the way of the world brings us death, not life. Life is only found by the way of Jesus Christ, the successor of life. Jesus succeeded in His life. He lived a perfectly sinless life though He was tempted as we are. He knows our weaknesses and has sympathy for us and helps us. And no temptation has overtaken us. God is faithful, and He will not allow us to be tempted beyond what we are able, He gives us a way of escape.

For we do not have a High Priest who cannot sympathize with our weaknesses, but was in all points tempted as we are, yet without sin. (Hebrews 4:15, NKJV)

For to this you were called, because Christ also suffered for us, leaving us an example, that you should follow His steps: "Who committed no sin, nor was deceit found in His mouth", who, when He was reviled, did not revile in return; when He suffered, He did not threaten, but committed Himself to Him who judges righteously; who Himself bore our sins in His own body on the tree, that we, having died to sin, might live for righteousness-by whose stripes you were healed. (1 Peter 2:21–24, NKJV)

No temptation has overtaken you except such as is common to man; but God is faithful, who will not allow you to be tempted beyond what you are able, but with the temptation will also make the way of escape, that you may be able to bear it. (1 Corinthians 10:13, NKJV)

So Where Is Your Mind?

If our mind is not in the Word of God, and it's in the world, this can lead to worldliness. We are where our mind is. Our mind controls who we are and what we do. If our mind is in the world, then we will be too. We will be a worldly people. But if our mind is in the Word of God, then we will be able to live by it, instead of the way of the world.

We will be a people who walk in the world by the Word! When I think of depression, it reminds me of defect. The word depression means a low place or surface, the state of being depressed or act of depressing; low spirits, gloominess; a period of severely *subnormal* economic activity. The word subnormal here is a key word that is defined to be below normal, less than the normal intelligence. If you ask me this is the defect.

The word defect means a fault; an imperfection; that which is lacking for completeness, fault; failing. So what's the defect in depression? Well, depression is a mind issue if you ask me. Most doctors will agree, the defect is in the brain. Depression affects people physically because the brain organ of thought and feeling is being affected by something. The drugs often prescribed to help people with depression affect the brain and neurological system because the brain is the controlling center of the nervous system. Sometimes most people often need more than one drug prescribed to relieve their symptoms, and it can be a very difficult thing to cure.

So what is it that the brain could really be effected by or lacking? You could do your own study of the brain on this, but I have studied and one thing I know is that I want the controlling of this person (me) to be based upon the word of God so that I can walk by it in the world. Again, if our mind is in the word of God, we will be able to live by it. When we lack the word of God in our life, we can become depressed and dimly lighted. Let's look at these words below that defines the diagnosis of depression.

1. *Gloominess.* What is it? It is being gloomy; imperfectly illuminated; dark; wearing the aspect of sorrow, *dejected, dismal, doleful.*

2. *Dejected:* Downcast, depressed, sad; sorrowful.

3. *Dismal:* dark; gloom; depressing; *melancholy;* depressed.

4. *Doleful:* full of causing grief, mournful; *melancholy.*

5. *Melancholy:* A state of despondency. esp. frequent or lengthy, *despondency, somber, contemplation.*

6. *Despondency:* to lose heart, courage, or hope, become depressed.

7. *Somber:* dark, shadowy, dimly lighted, dark and dull as color gloomy, depressing; serious or melancholy in appearance.

As we look at all the italicized words as defined, we can see some key words for the diagnosis of depression. These key words are sad, sorrowful, dark, gloomy, to lose heart, courage or hope, shadowy, dimly lighted, and dull. When we have the Word of God in our life, we don't feel like any of this because the Word of God gives us light and life. When our mind is in the word of God daily, it brings us life and lights our life. Knowing that God is light and gives light to every person coming into the world, and He is the source of our life supply and the length of our day's are in Him, we can know that God does not bring depression into our lives. When we lose heart of God then we can easily become dimly lighted, if you will, or depressed.

When this happens we really end up longing for God. We long for His love, and we seek His Light even though we might not know it. Ephesians 5:8 tells us that we were once darkness, but now we are light in the Lord. And now that we are light in the Lord, we should walk as children of light, not darkness. None of God's people should be sad, sorrowful, dark, gloomy, losing heart, courage, or hope, being dimly lighted and dull on a daily basis. Surely we have our days, but we also have our faith that He's given to each of us to walk in the world with.

When we have the Word of God in our lives on a daily basis, we live by it; we believe that the Word gives us joy, happiness, light, brightens our day, it cleanses our heart, gives us courage, hope, and life in all its fullness. Let's look again at the underlined word subnormal that links us to the defect.

#8 *Subnormal*—below normal, less than the normal intelligence. As I said, this word is key because it links us to the defect. We don't want to be lacking for completeness, we become complete in Him. We need the Word in our lives.

Your word is a lamp to my feet and a light to my path. (Psalm 119:105, NKJV)

There is lack of intelligence in the world, but not in the Word. What I mean is we shouldn't be subnormal, below the normal, or less than the normal intelligence. But we should be normal in relationship to the Word. The Word of God says that if we lack wisdom, we ask from Him, and He will give it to us.

> If any of you lacks wisdom, let him ask of God, who gives to all liberally and without reproach, and it will be given to him. (James 1:5–6, NKJV)

The wisdom we should be asking of Him is His Word. God gave us His Word so that we would be a people who have knowledge of Him. He wants us to be wise men and women, and if we want to be a people who come to completeness, then we have to turn back to the Word! We have to believe in Jesus, having patience walking in His own word's in the world. We have to set our eyes on Him to have understanding.

We shouldn't want the wisdom that comes from the world, but from the Word!

#9 *Defect* is defined as a fault; an imperfection that which is lacking for completeness fault; failing. The world is functioning on a subnormal level and that's why this links us to the defect, being the world is lacking for completeness. As I thought about depression, as I said it reminded me of defect. We can see here that the defect is the world is lacking for completeness.

The fault here is when a person doesn't have the Word of God in their life. This is why there is a lack of completeness, and we become dimly lighted and depressed. We need His Word in our life. He is the light and gives it to all, and it's all in the Word. Completeness comes with patience; it comes through Jesus Christ the Word.

> But let patience have its perfect work, that you may be perfect and complete, lacking nothing. (James 1:4, NKJV)

> and you are complete in Him, who is the head of all principality and power. (Colossians 2:10, NKJV)

The world doesn't have to be subnormal or lacking, because Jesus Christ, The Word of God, has come to us all as a light. See, Jesus Christ is the Light of the world, and we should no longer walk dimly lighted in the world, but walk as children of light. Put on the mind of Christ, read His word daily, believe in it, have patience as you walk in it. He is the Light of Life who will give you the light of life.

> Then Jesus spoke to them again saying, "I am the light of the world, He who follows Me shall not walk in darkness, but have the light of life." (John 8:12, NKJV)

> Let this mind be in you which was also in Christ Jesus, (Philippians 2:5, NKJV)

The Bible says, "In the beginning was the Word, and the Word was with God and the Word was God, He was in the beginning with God. All things were made through Him, and without Him nothing was made that was made. (John 1:1–3, NKJV).

Jesus is the Word that spoke *let there be light.* and we know there was light. Know that He is able to light your world!

> And God saw the light, that it was good; and God divided the light from the darkness (Genesis 1:4).

> "God called the light Day, and the darkness He called Night." So the evening and the morning were the first day (Genesis 1:5, NKJV).

God divides us from the kingdom of darkness when we are born into the kingdom of light. We become of the day so that we walk in the light, so shine your light! Fill your mind with the Word of God daily, your brain organ of thought and feeling won't be lacking anything that should affect your physical person's emotions or activity. Don't let depression rule your life, let the Word of God light your life. It is our faith that makes us well. Just believe in the Light, He will transform your darkness into light. It is important that if you are experiencing depression that you seek help, reach out to someone about it, reach out to God for His help, get into His word, and, if necessary, go to your doctor for help.

> Those who are wise shall shine like the brightness of the firmament, and those who turn many to righteousness like the stars forever and ever. (Daniel 12:3, NKJV)

We don't go for the least in life to get the most out of life. We have to reach for what is higher and above us to get success in life. We have to aim for the goal in life, to become everything that God has called us to be. God created us for a specific purpose, to give Him glory that He deserves. We have to step beyond ourselves and our plans to reach for what are God's plans for our life.

We will never succeed in life until there is an understanding that we have to succeed in the plans and purposes of God. People have said that successful living is when you live every day like it's your last. What does last mean when you are children of God? Our lives last forever. I live everyday knowing that He made me to last and for a purpose in Him. Each day to me is another day with a purpose in it and let's face it, anything less than God's purposes is living life at the least and will never be a life fulfilled purpose.

If we allow ourselves not to submit to the plans and purposes of God, then we submit to the opposition, being the lesser. The lesser is the enemy of life in which we choose death for our life. God wants us to have life, not death. The ways of the world are death, a life that will not be fulfilled, and it will have no meaning or direction. We can choose our path in life, either a path of darkness to death, or light to life!

> Do not enter the path of the wicked, and do not walk in the way of evil. Avoid it, do not travel on it; turn away from it and pass on. But the path of the just is like the shining sun, that shines ever brighter unto the perfect day. (Proverbs 4:14–15, 18, NKJV)

Jesus is the path to light and life as I've been saying. The other path is a path of darkness and in the end, death. Jesus is our Successor in life. He succeeded in fulfilling His purpose in life. It is because of this that we have life, and the path is opened to us into the Kingdom of God. We can bloom our way to success as Jesus did when we walk by His Word. While you are walking on the tracks, which is the right path, know that your steps will not be hindered. And also when you start to run the race, you will not stumble either.

> I have taught you in the way of wisdom; I have led you in right paths. When you walk, your steps will not be hindered, and when you run, you will not stumble. (Proverbs 4:11–12, NKJV)

Jesus is the door open to all our life supply. Everything we need in life is through Him. He hasn't hidden Himself from us, He is the One who opens the doors up for us and closes them. He knows what we need and when we need it.

An Abundant Life for You

Jesus came to give us an abundant life on earth and not only that, but in eternity also. The abundance Jesus gave us exceeds our life here on earth. I can't even imagine what's for us in heaven. If we are responsible of the lives God has given to us, then He will bless us with more. Of course, that means more responsibility for us also. Sometimes it seems like things go wrong and we don't feel like we have such an abundant life.

Well, the enemy steals kills and destroys, that is true, but Jesus came to give us an abundant life. He wants us to receive it!

> "The thief does not come except to steal, and kill, and destroy. I have come that they may have life, and that they may have it more abundantly. (John 10:10, NKJV)

Sometimes we rob ourselves from receiving the abundant life Jesus prepared for us. How? Well, we have to look at our life and see that what we have is God's, and He's let us borrow it. We have to see what we are doing with what belongs to God. Has it turned into anything? Have we been responsible with what God has given to us? Can we say look God, all that You have given to me and what I've done with it has multiplied.

See, if we are responsible over a little bit of what God has given to us, He will give us more. We have to set our heart, eyes, and desires on loving God and thanking Him for creation and what He has given to us. He's the Creator that created everything. When we are seeking God with our whole heart to love Him and are walking in obedience to His Word, and we are responsible with what's been given to us than we will experience abundance. Jesus wants us to receive all that He's come to give us.

It starts when we stop robbing ourselves of God's blessings. We have to give to God what belongs to Him, and what He asks of us. We should pay our tithes and offerings to the Lord. He's given us everything that we have. The 10 percent He asks of us is for His Kingdom's purposes, and whatever we offer extra is for His Kingdom's purposes. The first fruits of all of our increase belong to Him. He rewards and blesses the cheerful giver. If we do not give to Him what is His, we rob God and ourselves.

I don't know how many times I robbed myself until I learned the reality of this truth, but know that I don't like being robbed nor robbing God! I also know as I pay my tithes and offering's that the Lord is faithful to His word, and He does reward. We should seek first His kingdom.

> "But seek first the kingdom of God and His righteousness, and all these things shall be added to you. (Matthew 6:33, NKJV)

> "Will a man rob God? Yet you have robbed Me! But you say, 'In what way have we robbed You?' In tithes and offerings. You are cursed with a curse, For you have robbed Me, Even this whole nation. Bring all the tithes into the storehouse, That there may be food in My house, And try Me now in this," Says the Lord of hosts, "If I will not open for you the windows of heaven And pour out for you such blessing That there will not be room enough to receive it. (Malachi 3:8–10, NKJV)

> "The first of the firstfruits of your land you shall bring into the house of the Lord your God. You shall not boil a young goat in its mother's milk. (Exodus 23:19, NKJV)

> 'For to everyone who has, more will be given, and he will have abundance; but from him who does not have, even what he has will be taken away. (Matthew 25:29, NKJV)

As I said before, abundance does not just mean in this lifetime on earth, but also life in eternity with the Father. We must seek our treasures in heaven, not on earth. Truly we can receive abundance on earth, but it should never be treasured. Jesus should be our only treasure here on earth. And when we seek Him, we surely find treasure, and the treasure we seek should be of heaven.

> "Do not lay up for yourselves treasures on earth, where moth and rust destroy and where thieves break in and steal; "but lay up for yourselves treasures in heaven, where neither moth nor rust destroys and where thieves do not break in and steal. "For where your treasure is, there your heart will be also. (Matthew 6:19–21, NKJV)

> for so an entrance will be supplied to you abundantly into the everlasting kingdom of our Lord and Savior Jesus Christ. (2 Peter 1:11, NKJV)

We will all stand before the Lord on judgment day and tell the Lord what we've done with our lives. We should all hope to hear the words, "Well done, good and faithful servant; enter into the joy of your Lord."

> "For the kingdom of heaven is like a man traveling to a far country, who calls his own servants and delivered his goods to them. "After a long time the lord of those servants came and settled accounts with them. "So he who had received five talents came and brought five other talents, saying, 'Lord, you delivered to me five talents; look, I have gained five more talents besides them.' His lord said to him, 'Well done, good and faithful servant; you

were faithful over a few things, I will make you ruler over many things. Enter into the joy of your lord.'"
(Matthew 25:14, 19–21, NKJV)

There's good news. If we live our lives in accordance to the will of God, our reward will be great. And the good thing is, if we haven't been doing so great with what God has given to us, we can start doing great now. We can repent and turn to God and ask Him for help, and give to Him what belongs to Him that He may multiply what we have for His purposes. We can start the day anew because every day is a new day and new beginning. We don't have to wait for the day, we have to start now. It's not too late!

We can gain back and let God be in control of our lives. We can turn to Jesus and say,

Jesus, help me! And He will be there to help us through it all. He will help us; He wants to because He loves us, and He knows we can't do it on our own. He wants us to depend on Him and have the abundance that He has already given to us. We need to stop robbing ourselves. God has abundance for us!

> In Him also we have obtained an inheritance, being predestined according to the purpose of Him who works all things according to the council of His will,
> (Ephesians 1:11, NKJV)

The more we gain responsibility, the more we will receive. We will not achieve this alone however, man will always fail if man tries to do things man's ways. We have to turn to Jesus Christ the Word, and do things His way! Most of us have this mentality that the more we get, the more we want, and the less we heave, the more we want. No matter what, *we always want more.* But what we sometimes fail to realize is that we really only need (Jesus) the Word, and the Spirit.

We really need to seek His Kingdom first! Truly I tell you, the abundance I seek is of the fruit of the Spirit. I want an abundance of all the fruits that the Lord has for my supply to be able to give it to others. When we are born again, we are to carry a heavenly image—His image. We also have the Spirit in us that gives us the fruit we need for our lives and other people's lives.

We should be a people who should want the heavenly supply in the abundance that the Spirit gives. He gives it to us to walk in and give out! This is the abundance that I truly want in this lifetime here on the earth. People are hungry and in need, if we have abundance, then God will send us out to them. This is a treasure that a thief cannot come and steal, or moths and rust cannot destroy.

Where our treasure is, there our heart will be also. I want my treasure to be of His fruit in abundance, and there my heart will also be. I don't want what the world has. I want what the Word has! I want to drink from the fountain of life. How about you?

> On the last day, that great day of the feast, Jesus stood and cried out, saying, "If anyone thirsts, let him come to Me and drink. "He who believes in me, as the scripture has said, out of his heart will flow rivers of living water."(John 7:37–38, NKJV)

Holding Daddy's Hand

We've all stumbled and fallen from time to time. Even though we stumble and fall, we can't just stay down; we have to get up! We have to be the light that shines for others. We can't shine for others if we are down on the ground.

> "You are the light of the world. A city that is set on a hill cannot be hidden. "Nor do they light a lamp and put it under a basket, but on a lamp stand, and it gives light to all who are in the house. "Let your light so shine before men, that they may see your good works and glorify your Father in heaven. (Matthew 5:14–16, NKJV)

Jesus will always be there for us whenever we stumble and fall, He doesn't want us to stay down, He wants us to shine our lights so others will see it. He will help us get back on our feet; He will never leave us alone. He cares about everything that we go through and face. He's ready to help us whenever we turn to Him and ask Him for help. The truth is, He loves it when we depend on Him and ask Him for help, and not depend on ourselves.

We are never able, but the One is always able! We are acknowledging Him when we come to Him. We have to grab hold of everything we can in Jesus and stay on our feets, and keep our candles burning bright. Don't give up! He has His hand held out for us to grab hold of it. When Jesus was here on earth, He held onto His Daddy's hand, and He never let go of it. He is the light to all peoples.

We too have to be holding onto Daddy's hand to be a light that shines for the people also.

> "I, the Lord, have called You in righteousness, And will hold Your hand; I will keep You and give You as a covenant to the people, As a light to the Gentiles, to open blind eyes, To bring out prisoners from the

prison, Those who sit in darkness from the prison house. (Isaiah 42:6–7, NKJV)

Some of us are like a little child that was holding onto their daddy's hand, but something caught our attention, so we wandered away for a minute or two, and then discovered we left daddy's hand for a short time. We began to whine and cry for daddy to come back to us. The truth is, a child's father doesn't leave the child when the child's gone off to venture and discover something new. The child's father watches to see what his child is doing, why his child's wandered off. Our heavenly Father never leaves us either. We might feel like the child that thinks they're all alone and left, and maybe you began to whine and cry for Daddy, but Daddy's never left you. He never will!

> With a strong hand, and an outstretched arm, For His mercy endures forever; (Psalm 136:12, NKJV)

> Let your conduct be without covetousness; be content with such things as you have. For he himself has said, "I will never leave you nor forsake you." (Hebrews 13:5, NKJV)

Grab hold of His hand and don't let go! If a child wanders, it's okay. Usually the child's father or mother is nearby, watching and making sure they don't wander too far off. Daddy is always watching us to see if we are wandering and how far we wander. And He will be there if we get a little lost. He will pick us up and bring us back to Him.

Truthfully, if we are holding onto Daddy's hand, we will not likely wander from time to time and again. We will not find ourselves feeling left alone and start to whine and cry because we think that Daddy's left us. We will know that Daddy never left us nor forsook us; He has us in His hand always.

> Great peace have those who love your law, And nothing causes them to stumble. (Psalm 119:165, NKJV)

> Now to Him who is able to keep you from stumbling, and to present you faultless before the presence of His glory with exceeding joy, To God our Savior, Who alone is wise, Be glory and majesty, Dominion and power, Both now and forever. Amen. (Jude 1:24–25, NKJV)

> I have taught you in the way of wisdom; I have led you in right paths. When you walk, your steps will not be hindered, and when you run, you will not stumble. (Proverbs 4:11–12, NKJV)

6

The Prepared Kingdom

Seeing Life with
a Vision God Has Prepared

Life is seeing life with a vision God has prepared, using the eyes of the heart to hear

What's motivating you? When I think of deaf people, it amazes me how they hear. They hear with their eyes. When a person becomes deaf or is born deaf, they have to hear life in a new way by using their eyes. This is done by using sign language. Deaf people can see with their eyes, hand, and mouth movements allowing them to hear. Once a person has been born again, they have to hear life in a new way too so they can see the purposes of God in their lives. We have to hear what the Word is saying so we can see the world as He does.

What a person sees in the new way is not visible to them like it is for the deaf person who hears by using their eyes. What we see in the new way is spiritual/ invisible to us. So how do we see life in the spiritual new way? It's called faith. We received it from God.

> So then faith comes by hearing, and hearing by the word of God. (Romans 10:17, NKJV)

> Who through Him believe in God, who raised him from the dead and gave Him glory, so that your faith and hope are in God. (1 Peter 1:21, NKJV)

We needed faith before we were even born again. We needed the faith that came by hearing God's Word so that we could be born again. But now after our new birth, our whole life has to continue in faith. Our whole life has to become a walk of faith or a journey of faith. Faith is not something that we can see, but we have to have it to walk by and see life in a new way.

Basically we have to see with our faith that are the eyes of our heart. They are the eyes of our motivations. God has prepared a life vision for us to see. Mr. Luther King had a vision, we all should. We must know that God has given us a clear picture of life all around us to see. If we want to see it, we have to open the eyes of our heart up to it. We can't be walking by sight or what we see. We have to see and walk by faith. We have to see the picture (the world) and believe the Word and walk by it, we have to let it motivate us.

Remember, the worldview Adam and Eve first had was full of light, life, and goodness. They were a people moving about His Word in the world. And we know that when they disobeyed God, they now knew good and evil, and they not only saw the light, but also experienced the darkness. And we know Jesus Christ then came to us on earth as God in the flesh, and is the true and greatest light of the world for us all to see.

And He has given this light to every man coming into the world (see John 1:9). So now we have to see our worldview as God has restored it to us. That is: the focus of His Son being the center of the world where light, life, love, and goodness all comes from Him, the true Light of the world. We must focus on Him, the Light, and not the darkness. We must focus on the One who came to reconcile all back to Him.

Jesus shines through the darkness in the world. He has delivered us from the power of darkness. We must realize God has restored us! Receive what He has restored! He's given us authority over all the power of the enemy through Jesus Christ the Word, and as we shine our light, darkness cannot stand.

> "Behold, I give you the authority to trample on serpents and scorpions, and over all the power of the enemy, and nothing shall by any means hurt you. (Luke 10:19, NKJV)

> "Most assuredly, I say to you, he who believes in Me, the works that I do he will do also; and greater works than these he will do, because I go to My Father. (John 14:12, NKJV)

If we want to see the vision God has prepared, then we must focus on what He has given for us to focus on. That is Jesus, who will open up the clear picture of life for us all to see. He is life, and if we want the clear picture of life, we must turn to the One who gives us life! The deaf people in the world don't have a choice to close their ears up to the world, but with their eyes they can turn their eyes away from what they see because what they see is what they'll hear. Even the blind can't see the corruption in the world, but they can hear it. They too can close their ears to the corruption and function totally from the heart. And we too can be like the deaf who turn their eyes away from what is corrupt, and the blind who close their ears to what is corrupt so that we can see and hear the truth.

Jesus said His Words are truth and life. We have to turn to the Word if we want the truth. We need to open up our hearts and function by the seed that was planted in our hearts from His Word. When we open the eyes of our heart, He will speak to our heart, and we will be able to hear the vision God has prepared for our lives—that is the truth. When we are born again we are able to hear God speak to us because we are born of heaven and received His Spirit in us.

Deaf people can open their eyes to what is good and close their eyes to what is corrupt and their body can become full of light and ours can too. The blind who can't even see can become full of light too when they tune in their ears to hear the Word of God and open the eyes of their heart and see with the heart. We can too. With God all things are possible for Him who believes, and He's made a way for us all to view it the same. It's by our heart. See, our heart sees better than we do with our own eyes. What we see with our heart is God speaking to our heart.

—⁓∽০ᘏৎ⦿ᘏৎ০∽ᘏ—

Turn to the Headlight

Our human eyes can be like low beam headlights in the world that can't see through the darkness in the world. If we move with this light that is dimly lighted, then we can't get very far because we can't get a clear view. We have to have our eyes planted in the Word. We have to turn to the headlight that is the light that comes from Him, and let the headlight be in us. He will be the light for us that shines through the darkness. When our eyes are on the headlight, we will be full of light too. He is the word of God. He is the light. We are not going to make it with low beam headlights in a dark world, and we need the brightest on! Our eyes will no longer be dim lit or low beam. The light will enable us to see the clear view that will get us moving.

We'll be able to reach our final destination because the light will lead us through. God has given us His view to see the world. God wants us to know how He sees the world. If we want to know what He sees then we must turn to Him for the view of the world and not look in the world itself for the answers. If we do, then we will only see a worldly view of life, and it won't be a pretty picture concerning what's going on in it. It will definitely affect our heart, and our heart might even become hardened to the world. We have to open up our hearts to see what God is saying concerning the world. It's not by opening up ourselves to the world and hear what the world is saying.

It's about our heart, what's motivating us, that gets affected by what God is speaking to us concerning the world. What we will see when we open up our hearts is God's love for the world.

It is a beautiful picture. Our thoughts and motivations will get affected because the Word of God will have been planted as a seed in our hearts when He spoke to us, and that seed will be for the world once it matures. The seed of the Word of God that He spoke to us will grow as He continues to water it by His Words that will bring it to life. And what God grew in us will manifest itself then on the outside of us by our actions to the world.

It will be actions that we have to act towards the world, which is based on God's Word and His plans, and purpose in the world. We will be able to make a difference in the changing world as God sees it. This is what will get into our hearts when God speaks to us. It will be His love for the world in need of it. We need a worldview founded on the Word and not based upon the world. The truth is we all see the picture, we all get to view it, but we don't all view it the same.

We need the right heart attitude to view it. The right heart attitude says, "I feel God's love for the world, and it's beautiful, and I want to walk according to His Word and His plans, and His purpose in it." This is the heart that's listening to God speak. See it's about walking in His Word in the world. We must have faith to do it. We must walk by faith and not by sight.

We have to have faith and open up our hearts! Let's turn to the headlight and set our eyes on the Word and walk in His light in the world. See the world we view isn't going to change until our worldview does. Jesus Christ already has come to change the world; people just need to know it! The darkness cannot exist when the light shines! We all need to set our eyes on Him and get our lights shining in the world!

"And I have declared to them Your name, and will declare it, that the love with which You loved Me may be in them, and I in them."(John 17:26, NKJV)

See Jesus wants to be in all of us, and His love in all of us. We have to accept the change if we want the world to change! Jesus Christ is already the change in the world; our job is to shine our lights! The world needs to accept Jesus in order to change. He came to change us. So why is our world still living in the darkness when the light has come to us? The world lives by example, we need to be the example for the world to follow that are of His footsteps in the world! Walk in His path to righteousness!

We have to walk according to His Word in the world. We must know what He is saying about the world in which we all live, and must not see or hear what the world itself is saying to us. If we do, then the wrong seed will be planted, and that is the seed of the world. It too can be planted in our hearts, and it's a weed that will not bring life to others, just as a weed keeps life from the other plants close by it. And the world will water this weed with its corruption and that weed will never mature.

God has chosen deliverers to be sent to deliver people, and people are waiting right now for the deliverers to be sent to them. We have to take the step of faith and walk in all His ways and fulfill our calling in this life. People are waiting right now for us. God is waiting right now for us! This is why He has given us His view to see, hear, feel, smell, touch, and taste the world through Him. He loves the world. How could He not love it? He created it, and all that is in it. He gave us His only Son to die for us. We must realize that it's time to work for what God calls us to in the world. Truly we are not just working for the people, but for the people and for God!

We will make no difference in this world with weeds in our heart. We need the seed that is planted by the word of God that will grow in us and bring life to others in need.

We will be a rooted people in God's Word, and be able to speak life into people who are in need of it.

> "a land for which the Lord your God cares; the eyes of the Lord your God are always on it, from the beginning of the year to the very end of the year. "Therefore you shall lay up these words of Mine in your heart and in your soul, and bind them as a sign on your hand, and they shall be as frontlets between your eyes. (Deuteronomy 11:12, 18, NKJV)

Aim to Please God!

See the word of God belongs in our heart and the soul receives it too as God feeds the soul by His love for us. Our hand will do the serving and giving service that reaches out to the world with His love just as Jesus did in the world.

> "For if you carefully keep all these commandments which I command you to do- to love the Lord your God, to walk in all His ways, and hold fast to Him- (Deuteronomy 11:22, NKJV)

We are to love Him and love them, we are to walk by the Word in the world.

> not with eyeservice, as men-pleasers, but as bondservants of Christ, doing the will of God from

the heart, with goodwill doing service, as to the Lord, and not to men. (Ephesians 6:6–7, NKJV)

And whatever you do, do it heartily, as to the Lord and not to men, knowing that from the Lord you will receive the reward of the inheritance; for you serve the Lord Christ. (Colossians 3:23–24, NKJV)

We are aiming to please God only and give Him glory! We have to see the world from our heart as God speaks to it so that we can reach people. We serve them as we are serving God from our heart. We have to have the right heart attitude. This is why we can't let the world itself speak to our heart or walk by sight, because we will get a wrong heart attitude and won't be able to give God's love to people as God wants us to. We must plant our eyes on the Lord Jesus Christ and let Him affect our heart. Let's plant our eyes in the word of God. It is a holy, living, and powerful Word, and it will bring life and light!

My son, give attention to My words; Incline your ear to My sayings. Do not let them depart from your eyes; Keep them in the midst of your heart; For they are life to those who find them, And health to all their flesh. Let your eyes look straight ahead, And your eyelids look right before you. (Proverbs 4:20–22, 25, NKJV)

Receive, please, instruction from His mouth, and lay up His word in your heart. (Job 22:22, NKJV)

Blessed are the undefiled in the way, Who walk in the law of the Lord! Blessed are those who keep His testimonies, Who seek Him with the whole heart!

They do no iniquity, They walk in His ways. (Psalm 119:1–3, NKJV)

If we want to help people, we need His words in our heart! God sees it all. Even to the end, we have to walk by faith and believe for what is not seen to us by our sight.

For we walk by faith, not by sight. (2 Corinthians 5:7, NKJV)

God will speak to our heart concerning the world that He's spoken, God has big plans, and we are all a part of them. Let's all open up our heart and let God speak to us and walk in faith so that we can fulfill all that God has planned.

Life is the dawn of a new day, knowing that He's directing our every step of the way.

He will make your righteousness shine like the dawn, the justice of your cause like the noonday sun. (Psalm 37:6, NIV)

For with You is the fountain of life; In Your light we see light. (Psalm 36:9, NKJV)

There's something about the sun that draws us to it. We seek its light and the same is true about the true light that we seek, the Son of God who is the light of the world. We're drawn to the Son by His light. We live in a day when people want to be young and stay young as never before. We seek age defining products and care more about our youth and preserving it.

Why aren't we all looking for Him? He is there waiting for us to turn to Him and receive Him. Everyone is always talking about the fountain of life. Where is it? Was there one? Is there one? I wish there was one? We have to know about the Good News, Jesus is the fountain of life. It's in His light we see light and find life.

> On the last day, the great day of the feast, Jesus stood and cried out, saying, "If anyone thirsts, let him come to Me and drink. He who believes in Me, as the Scripture has said, out of his heart will flow rivers of living water." (John 7:37–38, NKJV)

> "but whoever drinks of the water that I shall give him will never thirst. But the water that I shall give him will become in him a fountain of water springing up into everlast-ing life." (John 4:14, NKJV)

Each morning is like no other. As we look out at the dawning of the new day to begin, it's so beautiful and really a piece of time that we will never be able to see exactly the same way again. It's amazing how the rising of the sun can be so different and beautiful every day. It also amazes me how Father raised His Son, Jesus, how He was so different and perfect, and how beautiful it is that He opened up the path of life to us. Every day is the end of one day and the beginning of the next. A day is 24 hours full of life, experience, and fulfillment.

It's 24 hours of life waiting to be experienced and fulfilled with meaning and purpose. The weather sort of directs how we are going to spend our day. We are always counting on the bright sun to shine throughout the day. In every season and all our events planned, we count on the sun to brighten up our day. The sun just seems to make us feel better inside, and it seems to make us more joyful in our day.

It seems like we do more with our time; it's like we get more strength. It is also true how Jesus directs our every step. We can always count on Jesus to shine upon us and in us to brighten up our day in any season of life that we go through. We realize that being born-again, we have the light in us to shine upon others. An effective and purposeful way that we can spend our time is to know that we are able to impart His light and love to others. We receive the greatest strength when we allow Jesus to work through us.

It's because of the Word and His love. See, love paints the picture. Love never ends. The Word gives us the clear picture. As I said, love paints the picture; the picture we see is our world that He's spoken into being because He loves us. His love is what never ends; it's because He loves us that we have something to look out at and see. He's the Word that gives us the view, it's because of Jesus that we are able to receive it.

> This is the day that the Lord has made we will rejoice and be glad in it. (Psalm 118:24, NKJV)

> "You are worthy, O Lord, To receive glory and honor and power; For you created all things, And by Your will they exist and were created." (Revelation 4:11, NKJV)

Sing it loud and sing it proud to Him who created it all for us to view it. You've got the view of the picture. Now let's get walking in it. Reach the world by walking in the demonstration of His life, light, and love for mankind. Walk in the Spirit!

Seek First the Kingdom of God

People say home is where the heart is. So where is your heart? Does it connect with His? Do you love the Lord God with all your heart, soul, mind, and strength? Are you keeping His Word? When we connect with God's heart and keep His Word, God's home is where our heart is. The Father is in Him, and He is in the Father; we are in Him, and He is in us, we are one with Him. God wants to make His home in you. He wants to connect with your heart. When God comes to make His home in us, He brings His kingdom with Him; the kingdom of God is within us see (Luke 17:21). How cool is that? Way cool! His home is in our heart, and if your heart is connected to His, then your home will be there also. We are a holy temple where He dwells and we have to keep our temples holy because God dwells in a holy place. Connect with His heart and keep His word! He went to prepare a place for us so that where He is, there we may be also. He's with us forever, and we are with Him forever. Do you know what kingdom you represent? What kingdom are you living for? We live in the kingdom of light. He's called us sons and daughters, to walk in His Light. The Light in us represents His kingdom where the King reigns in us! Seek first the kingdom of God!

> "that they may be one, as You, Father, are in Me, and I in You; that they also may be one in Us, that the world may believe that You sent Me. "I in them, and You in Me; that they may be made perfect in one,

and that the world may know that You have sent Me, and I have loved them as You have loved Me. (John 17:21, 23, NKJV)

Or do you not know that your body is the temple of the Holy Spirit who is in you, whom you have from God, and you are not your own? For you were bought at a price; therefore glorify God in your body and in your spirit, which are God's. (1 Corinthians 6:19–20, NKJV)

"He who has My commandments and keeps them, it is he who loves Me. And he who loves Me will be loved by My Father, and I will love him and manifest Myself to him." Jesus answered and said to him, "If anyone loves Me, he will keep My word; and My Father will love him, and We will come to him and make Our home with him." (John 14:21, 23, NKJV)

And this is His commandment: that we should believe on the name of His son Jesus Christ and love one another, as He gave us commandment. Now he who keeps His commandments abides in Him, and He in him. And by this we know that He abides in us, by the Spirit whom He has given us. (1 John 3:23–24, NKJV)

By this we know that we abide in Him, and He in us, because He has given us of His Spirit. (1 John 4:13, NKJV)

The world is in darkness and depression, but a light still shines to brighten them all up. People are down and gloomy just waiting for the light to shine upon them.

We can impart His light to others because He's in us and gives Himself to us to be with us. I thank the Lord in the morning, even when the sun doesn't shine, that He has given His Son—the true and greatest light—to shine upon us and in us and through us. It's the feeling we receive of His unconditional love for the world. He loves us enough that He gives Himself to us.

His light is in us. A light of life and love. Jesus is the reason that we shine. It's His light! What an amazing gift. Live a life of light and love. No longer are His children in darkness. What a transformation that we've gone from darkness to light. We are drawn to the Son by His light just like the natural light. We have to reflect His light in the world!

> For you were once darkness, but now you are light in the Lord. Walk as children of light. (Ephesians 5:8, NKJV)

> "While you have the light, believe in the light, that you may become sons of light." (John 12:36, NKJV)

Just like the natural world went from darkness to light in the beginning from creation— because the Light of heaven and earth created the light upon the earth and is the light in the earth, see, our day will end—but it doesn't have to end in darkness anymore. We can rest in the life and light He's given to us! Praise God! Light was divided from the darkness. We are born into the light. We are not part of the darkness anymore. We must continue in the light, and not become divided against ourself, if we become divided against ourself we cannot stand. We can't be both darkness and light, only one. He called us out of darkness into light, and His kingdom stands forever!

> But Jesus knew their thoughts, and said to them: "Every kingdom divided against itself is brought to desolation, and every city or house divided against itself will not stand. (Matthew 12:25, NKJV)

> But you are a chosen generation, a royal priesthood, a holy nation, His own special people, that you may proclaim the praises of Him who called you out of darkness into His marvelous light; (1 Peter 2:9, NKJV)

> 'And you shall be to Me a kingdom of priests and a holy nation." These are the words which you shall speak to the children of Israel.'" (Exodus 19:6, NKJV)

> How great are His signs, And how mighty His wonders! His kingdom is an everlasting kingdom, And His domain is from generation to generation. (Daniel 4:3, NKJV)

He prepared this kingdom from the foundation of the world for us! He called us into it that we shall reign forever and ever. Let's not forget that! The King reigns in us. He is The Light of Life who shines in our hearts in the world and gives glory to God.

> Now after John was put in prison, Jesus came to Galilee, preaching the gospel of the kingdom of God, and saying, "The time is fulfilled, and the kingdom of God is at hand. Repent, and believe in the gospel." (Mark 1:14–15, NKJV)

"Then the King will say to those on His right hand, 'Come, you blessed of My Father, inherit the kingdom prepared for you from the foundation of the world: (Matthew 25:34, NKJV)

There shall be no night there: They need no lamp nor light of the sun, for the Lord God gives them light. And they shall reign forever and ever. (Revelation 22:5, NKJV)

7

A Life Purpose Prepared to Fill

Life is having a purpose prepared to fill, following the voice of the Lord so still.

Each one of us has been created with a purpose prepared to fill; our job is to fulfill it. We became to become! We will become all that God has called us to be by following the Lord Jesus Christ and listening to His voice that is a gentle still voice, believing His word, holding it in our heart, loving Him, and being patient as He brings it all to past. He's already said it, and it will all become! His purposes do prevail! His words do not return to Him empty, they return to Him fulfilled!

Jesus came to the earth as truly God, and truly Man and He had a purpose prepared to fill before creation.

> He was chosen before the creation of the world, but was revealed in these last times for your sake. Through him you believe in God, who raised him from the dead and glorified Him, and so your faith and hope are in God. (1 Peter 1:20–21, NIV)

We too have a purpose prepared to fill that God has chosen for us before time began. God had a plan before He started to create! He planned it all before time began! God chose us from the beginning for salvation and called us by His Gospel. He's called us with a holy calling, according to His own purpose, given to us in Christ Jesus, before time began. He chose us in Him before the foundation of the world, to be holy, to be blameless before Him, to be His working man for good works to walk in which God prepared beforehand.

That's what we are—chosen and full of purpose! We each have something to do for Him!

> But we are bound to give thanks to God always for you, brethren beloved by the Lord, because God from the beginning chose you for salvation through sanctification by the Spirit and belief in the truth, to which He called you by our gospel, for the obtaining of the glory of our Lord Jesus Christ. (2 Thessalonians 2:13–14, NKJV)

> who has saved us and called us with a holy calling, not according to our works, but according to His own purpose and grace which was given to us in Christ Jesus before time began, (2 Timothy 1:9, NKJV)

just as He chose us in Him before the foundation
of the world, that we should be holy and without
blame before Him in love, (Ephesians 1:4, NKJV)

For we are His workmanship, created in Christ Jesus
for good works, which God prepared beforehand
that we should walk in them. (Ephesians 2:10, NKJV)

If you were the creator, wouldn't you have a plan before
you started to create? Think about it. When you start to
create something, don't you first plan it out? Why would
you even create it if you didn't have a plan or purpose for
it? God has a purpose for His plans. He created and is
watching it all being fulfilled to the end! You are part of the
fulfillment of what He's made, you know?

Aren't you going to fulfill what He's made you for?
That's what He's waiting for. Jesus was able to fulfill His
purpose in life because He loves His Father and mankind.
Jesus listened to His Father and obeyed Him.

By this we know love, because He laid down His
own life for us. And we also ought to lay down our
lives for the brethren. (1 John 3:16, NKJV)

"But that the world may know that I love the Father,
and as the Father gave Me commandment, so I do.
Arise, and let us go from here. (John 14:31, NKJV)

We know that Jesus obeyed His Father's plan for His
life and fulfilled His purpose in love. He loves His Father,
and He loves us. He let love rule in His life; it always
motivated His decisions. Now Jesus wants us to do the
same to fulfill it in love, we have to love also and let love

rule in our lives. Now I challenge you to set aside what you have planned and reach for what He has planned!

He already gave you the victory so go forth! Lay down your life for the Father and others in love. As God the Father sent His Son Jesus into the world, Jesus has sent us into the world, and through Jesus Christ all people can be saved. When we walk as Jesus did in the world others will see the light and the light will lead them to Jesus Christ the Lord and Savior of the world. The Light in us represents His kingdom where the King reigns in us! The kingdom of God is within us! The kingdom of God is the rule and reign of God in you!

> "As You sent Me into the world, I also have sent them into the world. (John 17:18, NKJV)

> So Jesus said to them again, "Peace to you! As the Father has sent Me. I also send you." (John 20:21, NKJV)

> "You are the light of the world. A city that is set on a hill cannot be hidden. (Matthew 5:14, NKJV)

> nor will they say, 'See here!' or 'See there!' For indeed, the kingdom of God is within you." (Luke 17:21, NKJV)

We all have an ultimate purpose in life—to become light and to arise and shine for the glory of God! Jesus glorified His Father; we can give glory to God too. When we listen and obey the voice of the Lord God Almighty, we can fulfill what God has planned for our lives, which is to give God glory that He deserves. As we all come together as a light that shines in the world, we'll be like a city set on a hill that cannot be hidden. How we fulfill our purpose in life only works one way—God's way!

Jesus Christ is returning for a shining bride who's made herself ready! Because God created us, we must turn to Him for our purpose in this world. God is who we need to have our eyes and ears tuned into, our individual purpose in this world is based on what He had to say. What He had to say was first planned by Him before time began, and then He said so and we became so. We need to know what the Word has to say.

It's all about the Word and not all about the world. Knowing that we were created with a purpose and an assignment is exciting news for us all. The excitement becomes greater once we've fulfilled it. We all want to fulfill our purpose in life, then we all have to obey the Father's plan for our life just as Jesus did. Jesus suffered, we will too. We will not suffer alone however.

> Yet if anyone suffers as a Christian, let him not be ashamed, but let him glorify God in this matter. (1 Peter 4:16, NKJV)

> Therefore do not be ashamed of the testimony of our Lord, nor of me His prisoner, but share with me in the sufferings for the gospel according to the power of God, (2 Timothy 1:8, NKJV)

> For to this you were called, because Christ also suffered for us, leaving us an example, that we should follow in His footsteps: "Who committed no sin, Nor was deceit found in His mouth", (1 Peter 2:21–22, NKJV)

and if children, then heirs- heirs of God and joint
heirs with Christ, if indeed we suffer with Him, that
we may also be glorified together. For I consider that
the sufferings of this present time are not worthy to be
compared with the glory which shall be revealed in us.
(Romans 8:17–18, NKJV)

It was no easy thing what Jesus faced for us. It will not
be an easy thing for us either, but we are not alone. We
can do all things through Jesus Christ who strengthens us.
Whenever we get weak and frail, it is then that He will
prevail. The good thing is that God is on our side, we must
not fear.

Fear will keep us from moving forward. We must know
that we can overcome with great faith and that God has
given us victory to overcome the world. We don't need to
try and figure out His plan for our lives. He's already said
so, and we already became so. All we have to do is love Him,
seek first His kingdom, walk in His Word giving Him the
honor and the glory, and we will become so. Just do good,
walk in all of His ways, keep His word in your heart, set
your eyes on Him, and shine bright for Him. When you
sin, repent, and when someone sin's against you, forgive and
pray for them. Keep your hands clean and willing, He will
put them to use.

I think our hands are the most beautiful thing that
God made on our body. Our hands hold a lot of what God
purposed us for. Be obedient and believe what He tells you.
Walk in faith as you make your laps in life. Don't rob Him
of what is His, pay your tithes, and bring your offerings to
Him. He got us to the starting line and will get us to the
shining finishing line.

For whatever is born of God overcomes the world. And this is the victory that has overcome the world- our faith. (1 John 5:4, NKJV)

And we know that all things work together for good to those who love God, to those who are the called according to His purpose. (Romans 8:28, NKJV)

———

In His Presence

Jesus doesn't want us to ever let Him go. No matter what we face, we can overcome when Jesus Christ strengthens us. Sometimes that means we have to get weaker first. This weakness will only produce strength in us. We get strength because He works in us and for us.

Whenever I become weak, I just lie down and rest. Whenever I become weak and want to rest it is not so that I can sleep the weakness away, but to get more strength. It's so that I can go to the Lord and receive something from Him. I want to rest in His presence and receive all that God has for my life. I close my eyes and see myself laying at the Lord's feet and not wanting to get up until I've received what God has for me. I see myself holding onto the hem of His garments and not letting go. He is my Comforter. He is where my comfort zone is.

I know He loves me, and I love Him. I don't let go till He blesses me. This is the feeling I receive in knowing Him—He is the living Word of God. I know that this is not just an imaginary place where I go to meet the Lord and lay, and rest in His presence. I know that I can reach Him; I know that you can too.

We must know that we can receive something from the Lord. We can truly reach Him and feel His presence. He is God with us! This is peace. This is rest. This is love. He is Jesus, the only begotten of the Father full of grace and truth. It reminds me of this piece of history in the Bible:

> Now a woman, having a flow of blood for twelve years, who had spent all her livelihood on physicians and could not be healed by any, came from behind and touched the border of His garment. And immediately her flow of blood stopped.
>
> And Jesus said, "Who touched Me?"
>
> When all denied it, Peter and those with him said, "Master, the multitudes throng and press You, and You say, 'Who touched Me?'"
>
> But Jesus said, "Somebody touched Me, for I perceived power going out from Me." Now when the woman saw that she was not hidden, she came trembling; and falling down before Him, she declared to Him in the presence of all the people the reason she had touched Him and how she was healed immediately.
>
> And He said to her, "Daughter, be of good cheer; your faith has made you well. Go in peace." (Luke 8:43–48, NKJV)

This was a great thing for this woman to experience. See, she was healed immediately when she touched only the border of Jesus' garment. This was possible for her because she believed, and Jesus even said to her to go in peace. It will only be possible for us to receive from the Lord when we have faith to believe we will receive from the Lord. Jesus is not distant from us at all. He's God with us! He is everywhere we need Him to be whenever we need Him to be. He's with us! We must believe that He is reachable and able to do all things, and we must believe this if we want what God has for us to receive of Him. As much as I love resting at the Lord's feet, I know that I can't all day. Jesus wants us to come to a place where we can be the mature people that He's called us to be. It doesn't mean that we're not mature if we rest at His feet, it just means that He wants us to stand strong in Him and reach people who are in need of Him.

I could lay and rest at the Lord's feet all day long; you could too. But He's given us work to do, and if we want to get the job done, we have to get up sooner or later, better sooner so we can accomplish all that God has for His purposes. The day will come when we will all meet Jesus face-to-face. What a day that will be. I can imagine I won't be able to take my eyes off of Him. I can imagine saying thank You, Lord! Thank You that You loved me, that You were always there for me, that You never left me, that You taught me, that You corrected me, That You saved me, and that You chose me, Lord. You are Great and Mighty! Worthy are You, Lord!

Well, this is what I feel. I don't know what I'll actually say or do. I might just stand in awe of Him and just be in awe till I fall to the ground and worship Him! He is so awesome! what do you imagine? What do you see yourself doing when you see the Lord face-to-face? In the meantime, we can rest at His feet when we become weak and receive that touch from Him that will give us all the strength we need to get us going in fulfilling God's purpose.

> Blessed are those who have learned to acclaim you, who walk in the light of your presence, Lord. They rejoice in your name all day long; they celebrate your righteousness. For you are their glory and strength, and by your favor you exalt our horn. (Psalm 89:15–17 NIV)

I personally don't know why everyone is so crazy about celebrities. To me, they are just people like you and me. I don't see what the big deal is. Jesus is the only big deal to me, and personally, He's my celebrity. I can't wait to meet Him. He's the glorious One. He's the one who gets my attention and has all the fame; the fame is all in His name! The name above all other names: Jesus, the Son of God! The KING OF KINGS AND LORD OF LORDS!

I imagine myself following Him around everywhere He goes and always being by His side. I don't think of being a servant like being a slave, but of one who loves his master and does

His will; he serves Him with his whole heart.

Love Fulfills Its Purpose

Jesus is the light of the world; a light with His life purpose fulfilled.

The Word of God is powerful and full of purpose, and we know that God spoke and all of creation exists. It is by Him that all things consist and exist.

> He is the image of the invisible God, the firstborn over all creation. For by Him all things were created that are in heaven and that are on earth, visible and invisible, whether thrones or dominions or principalities or powers. All things were created through Him and for Him. And He is before all things, and in Him all things consist. (Colossians 1:15–17, NKJV)

"You are worthy, O Lord, To receive glory and honor and power; For You created all things, And by Your will they exist and were created." (Revelation 4:11, NKJV)

Jesus came to us as a light into a world full of darkness. He fulfilled His purpose! He has given us His light, He wants us to shine it bright so others who are in darkness can see it, and come to it too. Jesus is the light of life, the light that fulfilled its purpose in God. We need to shine the light that He's given to us and fulfill our purpose in God too.

Jesus light is so visible that it open's the blind's eyes and they see it.

To open blind eyes, to bring out prisoners from the prison, Those who sit in darkness from the prison house. (Isaiah 42:7, NKJV)

Once we've become a light, whenever we cross another person's path, we are able to shine the light of Jesus to them. We have to keep our eyes on Jesus, the light of the world, to keep ourselves lit. If our eyes are on the things of the world, then our light will not shine because we will be full of darkness. Our eyes are a lamp to our body. What we see with our eyes determines if we shine or not.

"The lamp of the body is the eye. If therefore your eye is good, your whole body will be full of light. "But if your eye is bad, your whole body will be full of darkness. If therefore the light that is in you is darkness, how great is that darkness! (Matthew 6:22–23, NKJV)

"No one, when he has lit a lamp, puts it in a secret place or under a basket, but on a lamp stand, that those who come in may see the light. "The lamp of the body is the eye. Therefore, when your eye is good, your whole body also is full of light. But when your eye is bad, your body also is full of darkness. "If then your whole body is full of light, having no part dark, the whole body will be full of light, as when the bright shining of a lamp gives you light." (Luke 11:33-34,36 NKJV)

"you are the light of the world. A city that is set on a hill cannot be hidden. "Nor do they light a lamp and put it under a basket, but on a lamp-stand, and it gives light to all who are in the house. "Let your light so shine before men, that they may see your good works and glorify your Father in heaven. (Matthew 5:14–16, NKJV)

As the word of God grows in our heart, we will grow, and what we will grow is a mature relationship with Jesus the Christ. It's from the growing relationship and His love that we fulfill our purpose in life. It's nothing we need to look for, He already has plans for your life. Just relax, they're good ones. He is a good God, and He rewards. He loves you, and what He wants from you is to love Him and grow with Him along the way. He has all the wisdom you'll ever need in life. He's the greatest teacher. His instructions are sure to be right and bring us life! We have to keep our eyes stayed on Him so others will be able to see the light, the light of life! Now that you have the Light, walk in the Light and become sons of the light and the day.

God created us the highest of His creation on earth to be a light also that we come together as His chosen people to sit as a city set on a hill that cannot be hidden, we will be glorious when He returns! You'll be walking in the light forever! We know that Jesus was always the Light, He came to us as the light and is the light in the world, now Jesus is sitting at the right hand of the Father in heaven, He's the light in eternity also and we will be walking in the light in eternity. Do you know that we never stop walking in the light! We will reign with God forever and ever!

> "You are the light of the world. A city that is set on a hill cannot be hidden. (Matthew 5:14, NKJV)

> The city had no need of the sun or of the moon to shine in it, for the glory of God illuminated it. The Lamb is its light. And the nations of those who are saved shall walk in its light, and the kings of the earth bring their glory and honor into it. (Revelation 21:23–24, NKJV)

> There shall be no night there; They need no lamp nor light of the sun, for the Lord God gives them light. And they shall reign forever and ever. (Revelation 22:5, NKJV)

What's at the Finishing Line?

Jesus is standing there waiting for us. He's the shining bridegroom whose waiting for His bride whose made herself ready, she's without spot or wrinkle. His members arrive and are joined with Him. It's like a bride coming down the aisle to meet her bridegroom. Jesus is shining in all His glory and the members of His body. Then they are joined as one!

that He might present her to Himself a glorious church, not having spot or wrinkle or any such thing, but that she should be holy and without blemish. (Ephesians 5:27, NKJV)

"Let us be glad and rejoice and give Him glory, for the marriage of the Lamb has come, and His wife has made herself ready." (Revelation 19:7, NKJV)

Vows made to You are binding upon me, O God; I will render praises to You, For You have delivered my soul from death. Have You not kept my feet from falling, That I may walk before God In the light of the living? (Psalm 56:12–13, NKJV)

Christ has delivered us from the bondages of corruption, you have the glorious liberty to be a child of the Most High God! The whole creation groans and labors with birth pangs together for us to be revealed! We must shine! We must believe that all things are possible for us, not because we believe in us, but because we believe in Him who's in us who's able to do all things. There's nothing wrong with believing in one's self, it's just that it's about believing in the One who is greater than all, who is able to accomplish all things according to His purposes. So shine like the Son for the glory of God!

because the creation itself also will be delivered from the bondages of corruption into the glorious liberty of the children of God. For we know that the whole creation groans and labors with birth pangs together until now. (Romans 8:21, 22, NKJV)

"You are the light of the world. A city that is set on a hill cannot be hidden. (Matthew 5:14, NKJV)

For it is the God who commanded light to shine out of darkness, who has shown in our hearts to give the light of the knowledge of the glory of God in the face of Jesus Christ. (2 Corinthians 4:6, NKJV)

Let us run with endurance the race that is set before us!

Walk In the Light

Evening comes, the morning is dew, a light shines, and the day is new,
A path leads the way. Follow the Light, walk in the Light. It shines in the night.
When you stumble and fall, He will pick you up.
Hold onto the light, hold onto Him tight,
Hold the light close in your heart; He doesn't want to be apart,
Then when evening comes, and the morning is dew,
The light will shine bright in you. It will shine in the night, and in the day,
It will shine down the path you walk each way.
It will shine onto others, and they will see the path that leads the way,
They can follow the light that shines in the night.
When they stumble and fall, He will pick them up too.
He will tell them, *hold onto the light, hold onto Me tight*,
Hold Me close in your heart. I don't want to be apart.
You know the way; you've walked in the light.
And I didn't let it go out, no, not in the night,
So keep burning bright, others need the Light,
Shine on them bright, you have the Light!